D0031288

a long line of cakes

Deborah Wiles

SCHOLASTIC PRESS / NEW YORK

All rights reserved. Published by Scholastic Press, an imprint of Scholastic
Inc., *Publishers since 1920*. SCHOLASTIC, SCHOLASTIC PRESS, and associated
logos are trademarks and/or registered trademarks of Scholastic Inc.

Library of Congress Cataloging-in-Publication Data available

ISBN 978-1-338-15049-0

10 9 8 7 6 5 4 3 2 1   18 19 20 21 22

Printed in the U.S.A.   23
First edition, September 2018

The text type was set in Legacy Serif ITC
Book design by Maeve Norton

For Three of the Sweetest Cakes
Ever Baked:

Olivia, Delaney, and Abigail

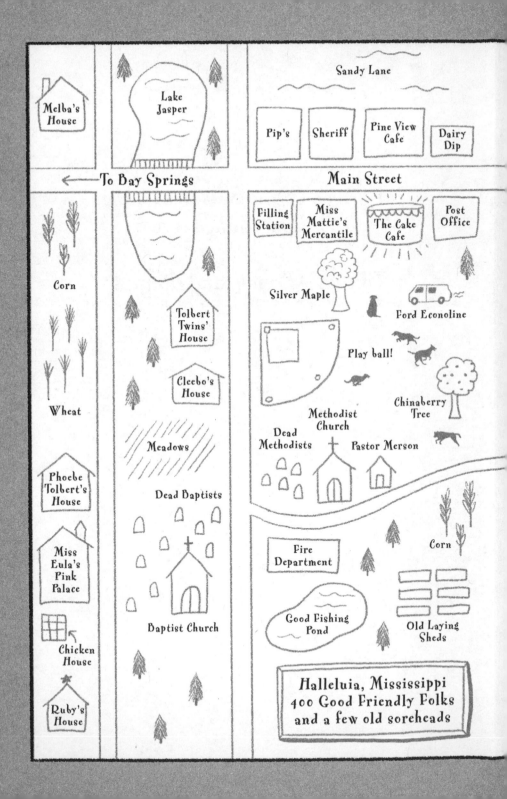

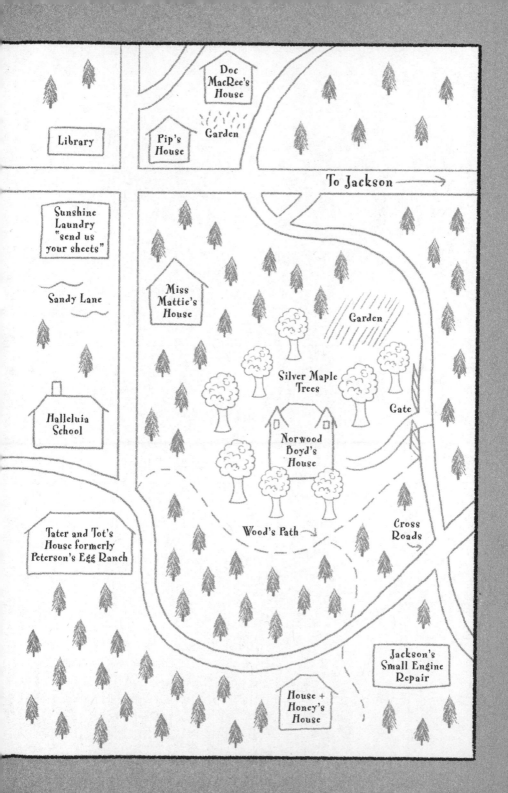

"It doesn't matter if it takes a
long time getting there;
the point is to have a destination."

—Eudora Welty

"...there is no place like home."

—Dorothy Gale

～ *Chapter One* ～

They came, like secrets, in the night.

The Cake Family:
Emma Alabama Lane Cake
Benjamin Lord Baltimore Cake
Jody Traditional Angel Food Cake
Van Chocolate Layer Cake
Roger Black Forest Cake
and
Gordon Ridiculously Easy No-Knead Sticky
    Buns Cake

Their parents were with them, of course:

Leo Meyer Lemon Cake
and
Arlouin Hummingbird Spice Cake

Somehow, there were also four dogs.

Thank goodness there was a suitcase rack on top of the car, and bicycle racks front and back. The Cake family had driven across the miles with the windows down, and everyone's hair was whisked to a froth.

The night air smelled like honeysuckle. A wispy fog rolled over and around the town as the Cakes arrived. It played leapfrog with the muggy summer air, just as that clever Cake fog always did. And then a cooler breeze, soft and snappy, began to dispatch the fog . . . just as it always did.

The breeze tickled the leaves of the majestic silver maple tree behind the post office on Main Street. Leo Cake turned the Ford Econoline onto the sandy lane that ran behind the post office and Miss Mattie's store. Their new bakery space—an imposing old structure—sat between those two buildings.

The radio was playing "King of the Road." King Leo Cake parked the car under the silver maple and leaned his forehead against the steering wheel.

"We're here," he said in a weary, dusty, long-time-traveling voice.

The car began to boil with boys trying to be the first to escape.

"Out of my way, birdbrains!" shouted twelve-year-old Ben. Lord Baltimore indeed.

The boys never noticed anything. Did they even notice they were moving their entire lives across the country—again? Emma Lane Cake wondered.

She was the only one, it seemed, who wanted to stay in one place.

"Already?" she'd asked her mother, when the packing had begun once again.

"We go when it's time," said Arlouin. "You know that."

"I know that I've moved seven times that I can remember," said Emma. "And more times that I can't."

"We suit up and we show up, Emma!" Leo Cake had told his daughter, with the delight in his voice that new beginnings always brought him. What was different this time for Leo was two lines of a poem that had floated into his head as they'd begun their trip:

Day by day and night by night we were together—
all else has long been forgotten by me

"Yes," he had answered the poem. Then, "No. I don't remember."

Now Emma's brothers and the dogs tumbled to the ground, a tangle of arms and legs stumbling over one another, glad to be *free-free-free* of their confinement and squash-ed-ness. Emma lingered in the space their absence created and stared at a knothole in the silver maple tree. Inside the knothole was a sliver of pink. A piece of paper? A secret note? She wanted to touch it.

A bright-orange moon shellacked the night. The boys

were giddy with the happiness that comes with finally arriving. Without speaking of it (which was how it usually worked), they had a plan. They raced across the sandy lane, turned their backs to Emma and their parents, and challenged one another to a peeing contest. Ben—always the ringleader—shouted, "Go!"

"Boys!" called Arlouin. "Mind your manners! There's a bathroom upstairs!"

"Aw, Mom!" whined Roger, only seven. "We couldn't wait!"

Emma, who was used to her brothers' shenanigans, got quietly out of the car and walked a few soft steps to the tree. The moonlight slid over her straight-as-a-stick brown hair and highlighted the spray of freckles across her nose.

The tree warmed to her touch. She felt its rough pulse under her fingers. It was the oddest feeling. She removed her hand and then put it back. There it was again, like a heartbeat. If trees could smile, this one would. She looked around her in wonder. Was she mistaken, or did everything about this town feel alive and waiting for her?

On tiptoe, she peered into the knothole of the silver maple. It *was* a note! Her fingers itched, wanting to tug on it.

"Quiet!" Arlouin shushed her boys, who were whooping and hollering through their contest. "It's midnight! You'll wake the dead!"

"No one lives on Main Street," said Leo. He put his arm around his wife. "Not even the dead."

"We passed two cemeteries on the way here!" shouted Jody in his high angel-food voice. Ten-year-old boys are practiced at being informative when necessary . . . and even when not.

"No one will hear us," Leo assured Arlouin. "And we've been cooped up for hours."

He used his index finger to push the bridge of his glasses up on his nose as he walked toward the boys. "Good idea," he said.

"I won!" shouted Jody.

Then Ben shoved Jody who shoved Van who shoved Roger, which made Gordon, the littlest Cake, cry. The dogs began to bark as they swirled around the shoving boys.

"Where's my baseball glove?" shouted Ben, in his Lord Baltimore voice. "I just had it!"

Jody—who was no angel—jumped like a frog and waved Ben's baseball glove in the air. "Keep away!" he shouted.

"I've got the ball!" cried Van in his thick chocolate-layer-cake voice, an unusually low voice for an eight-year-old.

"*We* live on Main Street now," said Arlouin as she swooped the wailing Gordon into her arms. "And we will mind our manners. Cakes always mind their manners. Boys! Bedtime!"

Leo was right. No one else lived on Main Street. Long ago people often lived above their stores in little Southern towns, but now people lived in houses of their own, away from Main Street. No one in Halleluia, Mississippi, saw them arrive, because it was midnight and everyone was tucked in bed, asleep—all four hundred good friendly folks, and a few old soreheads.

"Emma," said her exasperated mother, "take Gordon, please, while I round up the hooligans."

"Yes, ma'am."

Gordon, who at four years old wanted to be like the big boys, held out his reedy arms for his sister, his favorite. Emma's itchy-fingers spell was broken, and she smiled at her brother. "Come here, Sticky Buns," she said with a sigh.

"Emma," he sniffed. He tucked his head under her chin.

Emma's eleven-year-old arms were muscled from hauling bags of flour for the bakery and stirring so much soup for the lunches the Cake Café served every weekday. She could tote a twenty-five-pound bag of carrots all by herself. Her brother was as light as a cinnamon stick. Gordon wasn't built like her other brothers, who were as solid—and thickheaded—as baseballs.

The boys, relieved of balls, gloves, and full bladders, scuffled to the back of their new home between the post office and Miss Mattie's Mercantile. The last tendrils of fog and the breezy dark shadows of the silver maple played across its surface.

"It looks gothic," said Emma.

"It's haunted!" Jody declared with delight.

"I'm hungry!" said Van. He grabbed Roger's arm and pretended to eat it.

"Mom!" whined Roger.

"Shhh," said their mother.

There was a milk-box cooler by the back door, used for dairy home deliveries. Leo opened it to find a glass jar of milk, a clutch of eggs, and a pound of butter inside. "How thoughtful," he said.

Arlouin unlocked the tall red door with a long metal key. It turned with a solid *click* in the metal keyhole.

Emma gave the silver maple one last look before walking through the doorway of her new home. She imagined the note had been left for her. It was easy to imagine it when a tree had almost talked to you.

"What will we find in this new place!" Leo Cake crowed, suddenly revived. He loved the first moments of a new life in a new place. Everything was possible and nothing was spoiled. There was no disappointment. The world was born again, every time they stepped across a new threshold.

The door swung open. Their story began.

~ *Chapter Two* ~

Eight Cakes banged up the back stairs with their suitcases and dogs, and hurtled into their new beginning. They flipped on lights, carved out territory, and assessed their new living quarters.

"The movers will be here tomorrow with the kitchen equipment," said Leo.

Arlouin nodded. "The upstairs kitchen will do fine for now."

"There's only one bathroom!" yelled the boys.

"Emma goes first!" called their mother.

"I'm sure there's another downstairs," said their father.

"Bunk beds!" yelled Jody and Van. They began to argue over who got the top.

"Bunk beds!" whined Roger.

"It's a dorm room," said Ben.

"It's the living room," corrected Arlouin. "It will do nicely for five boys."

"It will be fine for now," said their father. "We're lucky to have this much room on such short notice."

"It *was* short notice," agreed Arlouin, which brought tears to Emma's eyes. She had hardly had time to say good-bye to her newest best friend, Annie, and she couldn't stop thinking about the loss.

The family's new-arrival fizz ran out quickly, and soon the Cakes settled themselves and fell quietly and gratefully asleep in the beds that had been waiting for them:

A cozy feather bed in the front bedroom facing Main Street for Leo and Arlouin.

Two sets of bunk beds for the boys and the dogs, in the living room. Gordon, sniffling, squished in with Roger, who was not happy about it, but was too tired to protest. "We'll figure it out tomorrow," said their dad.

And finally, a lopsided four-poster double bed with a soft old quilt for Emma, in her own small bedroom at the back of the building, facing the sandy lane.

Emma opened her window, snapped on the bedside lamp, and surveyed her new sleeping arrangements. This bed would be big enough to include Emma's brainy best friend, Harriet, the friend Emma had left behind when she was eight. It would be perfect for her fussy best friend, Evangeline, whom she'd left behind when she was nine, and her bookworm friend, Mariposa, whom she'd left behind when she was ten. It would even be big enough for the twins, silly Marcy and Drucy, whom she'd left behind when she was six. They had laughed at Emma's bad jokes, had praised her six-year-old drawings, and were the first friends to sample her very first attempt at making her now-famous chicken soup.

Emma lugged her suitcase onto the bed and snapped it open. On top of the shorts and shirts and shoes and pajamas and one good Sunday dress was her carefully rolled and rubber-banded *Map of the Known World and Friends, According to Emma Alabama Lane Cake*. That was its long name.

She had tried calling it her Friend Geography Map or just Geography Map for short, or Friend Map, but none of these seemed just-right. It wasn't a map in the topographical sense, anyway. It was more a record of her life, a periodical she occasionally published more of, just for herself, outlining and adding to the places she had lived, and the friends she had left in those places.

She had finally settled on calling it her Friend Atlas, which pleased her. The word *atlas* was perfect. She had learned it in Mrs. Forthright's class last year. She had arrived as a new student just before the maps-and-globes unit started, and had moved just after it ended, right in the middle of the explorers unit, scarcely twelve weeks later. It was as if the idea of atlases had been waiting for her at that school like a gift. She had changed the atlas definition to suit her purposes:

An atlas is a book or collection of maps and charts and pictures and drawings and lists and facts and history and stories about special places and people and things in your life. Especially friends.

Now, with the house quiet around her, room to move and breathe and think, and a tranquil breeze coming through the window, she sat on the bed, unrolled her

Friend Atlas, and tried not to cry as she pored over the special friends from each place she had lived. There was nothing like a best friend. And tonight, in this new place, she had none.

She put her Friend Atlas back in her suitcase and looked out the window at the silver maple in the moonlight. She heard a symphony of snoring from the living-room bed-room. Her brothers were numbskulls, but they had personality, she had to give them that. It was impossible not to like them. They would each have a new friend before breakfast. They knew they had no time to waste.

Neither do you. The thought came with a practical clarity she had never before experienced. It was as if the tree or the breeze were whispering to her, and the idea sounded so reasonable she allowed herself to believe it.

There would be little time, this time, said the tree, said the breeze, said her rational mind, for her usual careful consideration and selection of friends. But there might be a friend waiting for her in the knothole of that tree. *Hurry!*

Her heart began an excited thump-thump-thump in her chest.

She slid off the bed and dug her notebook and favorite pencil out of her satchel. By the bittersweet light of the moon she wrote a note, drew a little picture to go with the words, because that was her habit, folded the note twice, and tiptoed down the stairs and out to the silver maple tree.

She tucked her note inside the knothole, next to the pink one.

She looked around her in the dark. This place. *Maybe this place is finally the one. Maybe we can stay. Forever.*

Could she even allow herself to have such a thought? Of everyone in her family, she was the most levelheaded, pragmatic one.

But not tonight. The sweet-tempered breeze that had scattered the fog now eddied around Emma and whispered:

Yes.

Emma blinked. Then she said softly to the tree, to the breeze, to the noisy crickets who sang from the tall grass:

Please.

To Whom It May Concern,

I am cooking an interesting soup. Saturday afternoon. Please come.

Emma Alabama Lane Cake

THE AURORA COUNTY NEWS

BUSINESS PAGE

commandeered by Miss Phoebe "Scoop"
Tolbert while Ed Edwards is away on
vacation to New Orleans

In a surprise two-step turn of events in downtown Halleluia, Doc MacRee—who has always had more patients than he can shake a stick at—has cut his medical practice in half along with his office space. At the same time, Jerome Fountainbleu, owner of the Pine View Café, across the street from Doc MacRee's office, has announced the retirement of Misanthrope Watkins, also known as "Old Widow Watkins," who made the best coconut cream pie in the state of Mississippi.

"Lemon meringue, too," said Fountainbleu. "We don't know what we're going to do without her. Customers come just for our desserts. We may have to close."

This reporter knows that that sentiment is ridiculous. The Blue Plate Special at the Pine View Café is also famous county-wide and creates a line out the door at noon Wednesday, when fried chicken and butter peas are on the menu. There just must be something done about dessert.

Cornelia Ishee, known colloquially, locally, as Aunt Tot to most residents of Aurora County, volunteered at last night's Eastern Star meeting to take over in the pie-making department. There was general unrest from the assembled, as well as a murmur of "Not on your life" heard distinctly from the back row, although all present pretended they had heard nothing. I can faithfully report, however, that the voice definitely sounded like it belonged to Miss Mattie Perkins.

I see I am out of room. More about Doc MacRee in our next installment!

Yours faithfully, PT

～ *Chapter Three* ～

The sun was just pushing itself up and awake as Miss Mattie Perkins arrived at the back door of the Mercantile, next door to where the Cakes were sleeping. She was tired. Yesterday's 200th anniversary celebration for Aurora County had included a ball game, a pageant, and a Fourth of July picnic that had attracted people from the far reaches of the county, including folks she hadn't seen for years.

It had involved way too many people for her taste. She had given a short, heartfelt speech at the last, something she never did, but something she felt compelled to do to honor her friend Norwood Boyd, who had recently passed away. She had wanted to put the rumors to rest so everyone would just *go home.*

Now here she was, back at work again and way too early, considering how late a day yesterday had been.

The first yellow sun rays winked off the side mirror of the Ford Econoline parked under the silver maple tree. Miss Mattie took one look at the car, snapped out of yesterday, and said, "Humph! Eula!" She sailed into her store like a Viking wearing a horned helmet. She grabbed the telephone and dialed Miss Eula's number.

"You said you weren't going to do it!" she shouted into

the phone, without even a hello. "And now you've gone and done it! I should have known. Eula!"

"Good morning, Mattie!" said Miss Eula in a voice like sunshine itself.

"Don't you good morning me!" shouted Miss Mattie. "I told you I needed the space next door that Doc MacRee vacated so I can have more storage. I told you a dozen times!"

"I said I'd take it under consideration," said Miss Eula, more somber now.

"Well, consider again!" snapped Miss Mattie.

"It's my building, Mattie," Miss Eula said in an even voice. "Garnet left it to me."

"My brother never did have any good business sense," said Miss Mattie. "I thought you might develop some, being married to him for as long as you were. Heaven knows one of you needed it!"

For a beat, neither of them spoke. Then Miss Eula said, "Doc MacRee can't use the building anymore, Mattie. I can do with it whatever I like."

"I suppose that includes turning it into a summer camp!" said Miss Mattie. "There are seven bicycles strapped to the van out back. Seven!"

Miss Eula laughed. "This should be interesting!" she said. "We'll be right over! Although I arrived home only hours ago and I haven't seen Ruby yet."

"We?" Miss Mattie erupted. "Do *not* bring that

17

child! Do *not* bring those chickens! Do not, do you hear me? Do *not*!"

"You're about to have your hands full, Mattie," said Miss Eula. "You'll need all the help you can get!"

At just that moment, four boys carrying baseball gloves, a wooden bat, and one beat-up baseball came through the back door, hungry. They wore the clothes they'd gone to bed in, which were the clothes they'd had on all day the day before.

Miss Mattie slammed the phone on the counter.

"We're closed!" she snarled.

"We're hungry!" one of the boys said. "Our mom and dad are still sleeping! And we don't have any food!"

"What do you want me to do about that?" asked Miss Mattie, hands on her hips.

A fifth boy, a slip of a thing, came tiptoeing into the store. He looked at Miss Mattie with big round eyes. "Is this where the cereal is?" he asked in a timid voice. Behind him, outside the back screen door, four dogs whined and begged to come inside. They were hungry, too.

Ben snatched a box of oats from the shelf, in his twelve-year-old Lord Baltimore, ringleader way, and held it over his head. "*This* is cereal!" He beamed. He tossed it to ten-year-old Jody, who caught it in his glove and tossed it to eight-year-old Van, who tossed it to seven-year-old Roger, who dropped it. The box split open and rolled oats spilled all over Miss Mattie's clean wooden floor.

"Vaaan!" Roger whined. "You made me drop it!"

"Did not!" Van protested. "You're a butterfingers!"

Miss Mattie planted herself smack in front of Ben as if she was going to make a citizen's arrest and take Ben across Main Street to the sheriff's office herself, but then Gordon began to cry, which brought everything to a halt. Even Miss Mattie seemed to be deciding what to say.

Everyone stared at Gordon for a quiet moment, which made him stop crying. He sniffed. Then all eyes were on Miss Mattie.

Jody, suddenly angelic, said, "We could sweep it up. We have breakfast recipes at our house. We've got flour, sugar . . ."

Miss Mattie recovered herself. "This is a recipe for disaster," she said. "All of you! Out! And take that sniveling small creature—and those dogs—with you!" She winced as she said it, but she was firm. She could not afford nonsense like this on a Saturday morning, when the store would soon be full of customers. This was so much worse than she'd thought it could be.

Ben tucked his glove into his armpit. "Please don't be mad at Gordon, ma'am." He looked Miss Mattie in the eye—he was tall for his twelve years. "He can't help it."

The boy's manners impressed Miss Mattie, which was his intent.

"You stay," she said. "You should be a better example for him." She grabbed a broom and dustpan by the back door and shoved it at Ben. "Clean this up. You can work off what you owe for those oats."

"Ma'am?"

"You heard me. I have a whole list of chores you can do."

Ben blinked. "But—"

"But nothing, young man. Consider yourself indentured. Hand me that glove."

Ben relinquished his glove with a stricken look. He fervently hoped he'd get it back. He took the broom and the dustpan. His brothers banged away from Miss Mattie's back door as quickly as they could, screaming, *"A ball field!"* at the top of their lungs. Ben, miserable, watched them race across the sandy lane with the dogs, across a stretch of grass to the field where the Aurora County All-Stars played.

A ball field! A real ball field! Now that the sun was fully, gloriously shining, they couldn't miss it. The grass was dewy, the birds were singing, the shadows of night were gone. And Ben was stuck inside with Miss Mattie Perkins. She stared him down. He began to sweep. Oats were scattered everywhere.

"Don't miss a one," Miss Mattie snipped. "I pride myself on my spick-and-span floors."

She put Ben's glove on her long counter. She donned her work apron. She turned on all the lights and the big electric fan. It would be hot today. She turned the CLOSED sign in the front window to OPEN. She unlocked the double front doors and opened them wide so that the screen doors with the Sunbeam Bread signs would bring in a breeze all day. And that's when she was almost run over by a redheaded, ponytailed girl in blue overalls blowing through the double screen doors.

Ruby Lavender had arrived.

~ Chapter Four ~

"Oh, for pity's SAKE!" cried Miss Mattie.

But Ruby did not stop. This path through Miss Mattie's store was the shortest one to the silver maple tree, and she knew she had a note from Miss Eula in its knothole. "Good morning, Miss Mattie!" Ruby called as she ran by her great-aunt and straight through the store, past the barrel of crackers and the boxes of shoes and the wall of fabric and the refrigerated case of soda and milk and eggs and butter. She ran past the new sweeper, Benjamin Lord Baltimore Cake, without so much as noticing him. She was a girl on a mission.

"Who . . . ?" said Ben, but Ruby was already gone.

She pushed through the back screen door of the Mercantile and saw the boys playing baseball and the dogs running the bases with them. The sight made her stumble like a locomotive jumping its tracks. She picked herself up, brushed her unruly red hair out of her face, and ran across the sandy lane.

"Hey!" She waved her arms. "Hey! New kids!"

"You're out!" shouted Jody in his high, angelic voice.

"Am not!" shouted Van in his thick, chocolate voice.

Then the pushing started.

"Come *onnnn*!" whined Roger, the black cloud. "Can we find something to eat now?"

Gordon was practicing stag leaps back and forth over the third-base bag when he saw Ruby. He stopped to stare at this girl, just as the dogs found her—*somebody new!*—and swarmed around her, greeting her, *happy-happy-happy!*

"Good garden of peas!" said Ruby, laughing and patting all four dogs at once. The big black one snuggled under her arm for a hug. He looked so much like Dismay, Comfort Snowberger's lost dog. She gave him a squeeze and he kissed her. Ruby laughed, then yelled at the boys, "Who are you?"

"It's a girl!" screeched Gordon, and the boys stopped their scuffling. Jody, Van, and Roger ran, like a one-celled organism, to where this new girl stood. Gordon trailed behind them.

They stopped before they barreled over Ruby, who took a step backward as they caught their breath. They were smiling all over their faces. A new friend already.

Ruby opened her mouth to speak, but another voice interrupted her.

"Boys! Breakfast!" It was their mother, Arlouin, calling from the back door of their new home. She stepped off the stoop carrying an enormous basket—they recognized it, it was the muffin basket—and walked next door to the back door of Miss Mattie's store. She motioned to her

23

boys to join her. "Oatmeal raisin! Your favorites! Come on, let's meet the neighbors! Cakes always make good first impressions!"

A whiff of nutmeg laced with brown sugar filled the air. Everyone's stomach rumbled. Ruby stared from the wrinkled boys to their cheerful mother, while the dogs raced to the muffins to see if they might successfully beg for one.

"We can't go in there," whined Roger. "We're banned!"

"There's a crazy lady in there," warned Van.

"She took Ben hostage!" yelled Jody.

"That's nuts!" said Ruby.

She marched to the back door of the Mercantile and opened it. "Miss Mattie wouldn't hurt a gnat," she said. "And she's as sane as yesterday's news. Go on in."

Arlouin smiled. "Thank you, sweetheart."

Ruby corrected her. "I'm Ruby. And I'm not very sweet."

The boys watched their mother disappear inside the store.

"Go on in," Ruby told the boys. "I'll vouch for you. You play ball, you're all right."

The boys looked at this strange girl they hadn't met as they filed into Miss Mattie's store, their hunger overcoming their fear. Gordon even made a little hop over the threshold.

The dogs stayed outside with Ruby.

As much as she wanted to see what was going on inside the Mercantile, Ruby wanted her note more, and she had to retrieve it while no one was looking. She did not want to give away her hiding place.

She peered into the knothole of the silver maple and blinked in surprise.

"Two notes!" she whispered. She tucked them deep into her front overalls pocket. Before she could read them, she had some vouching to do. She'd better hurry up. She would meet these new boys, and she would have a muffin baked by their very nice mother. She'd bring some muffins out for the dogs, too. And she'd unwind the hose and fill a bucket with some water for them. Good thing she hadn't brought her chickens!

She looked around at the empty ball fields, the empty lane, and the empty town, this early in the morning. Who else in Aurora County would have written her a note?

She couldn't guess that the letter writer was directly above her, watching everything unfold from a second-story window and wondering how to introduce herself.

~ Chapter Five ~

Emma Lane Cake had helped her mother make the muffins. She had put on fresh clothes and combed her hair. She had kept watch on the silver maple tree.

And now, here was a girl in pink flip-flops and a sloppy ponytail, taking her note out of the knothole. Emma clasped her hands together at her chin. She could hardly contain her excitement. But on the heels of her happiness came thoughts about how it would once again hurt to leave new friends.

The best way to avoid hurt was to avoid making a friend, to avoid adding one more friend to her Friend Atlas. At some point, if she kept moving and adding friends, the atlas was going to be so big, one room and four walls wouldn't be able to hold it.

These were daytime thoughts, the kind of thoughts the light of the sun illuminated. In the soft dark, you could think anything was possible. Trees warmed at your touch. Breezes spoke. Making friends was a magical matter of leaving a note in a knothole. Ridiculous.

She had been wrong last night, in her moment of weakness, her moment of wanting something she knew she couldn't have without eventually hurting. And now it was too late to take her note out of that tree.

"Hey, Girl Scout," said her dad as he walked into the kitchen for coffee.

"Hey, Daddy."

"I smelled those muffins in my sleep!" Leo said as he rummaged in a box for a coffee cup. He pushed his glasses up on his nose as he looked.

"They're an exceptionally good batch," said Emma Lane Cake.

"They always are when you have a hand in making them." Leo squeezed her shoulder then gave it a pat as he moved from box to box.

"Never thought I'd see this town again," he mumbled.

Emma's scalp began to tingle. "You've been here before?"

"Long ago, I think. Or a town just like it." He gave her a half smile. "We never go anywhere twice. So if I was here before, I must have been passing through."

They were always passing through.

"Was I born then?" Emma asked, a wild sort of hope in her voice. Maybe that would explain the tree and the wind and her crazy feelings of *maybe this place is finally the one.*

"Let's see . . ." said her father. He rubbed the bottom of his chin with the backs of his fingers, because that was his habit.

"Yes. No. I don't remember."

"Daddy! How can you not remember?"

"I only remember today, potato pancake," he said in his absentminded and affectionate way. "And today, I need to

27

start a bakery!" He turned on the radio. A twangy old country tune spilled into the kitchen. "Boy, you can tell we're in the South again!" said Leo Cake.

He took his daughter's hands and started to whirl her around the kitchen, bumping into boxes, singing off-key: "How's about cookin' somethin' up with me?!"

Emma had to wait for the song—and dance—to end, and she laughed in spite of herself. But she wouldn't let her father change the subject.

"I think this might be *the* town, Daddy," she said.

"What town?"

"The town we settle in for good," Emma continued. "I had a thought about it, last night."

"What kind of thought?"

She couldn't say.

"We don't settle down, Emma," said Leo. We come from a long line—"

"—of itinerant bakers," Emma finished with him.

"Exactly," said her father, happy to have passed on the family history.

"But we *could* stay here!" said Emma. "Why not?"

Leo Cake gave his chest a thump. "Because!" he thundered. "We are Citizens of the World! And proud of it! That's what my father—Archibald Carrot Cake, Blue Ribbon Bona Fide Grand Champion Baker!—always told me, and it was good enough for me, growing up."

Emma knew *that* story. Archibald Cake took his young

son Leo with him to spread love and confectionery goodness all over the world, never going to the same town twice. When Emma was little, the story felt romantically delightful, especially as told by her fervently optimistic father.

But now that she was eleven, Emma was tired of it. She halved a muffin and stared at it. "We're from nowhere, then," she said.

Leo Cake used one finger to push up the nose of his glasses. He cleared his throat. "Emma Lane Cake!" he spouted. "Our line of itinerant bakers stretches from the Russian Steppes across Asia to Norway to Germany to Spain to England to the shores of the United States of America on boats like the *Mayflower*! Who do you think baked their bread, made their cake, kept them alive and well fed?"

But Emma had heard this speech before, too. She shook her head.

"We're *nomads*, Daddy. We have no home."

Her father shoved the peanut butter across the counter to Emma. "*This* is our home," he said with feeling. "For now."

"For how long?" Emma asked.

"For as long as it takes," her father said, as he always said, which meant nothing to Emma. Nothing. She slathered peanut butter on half a muffin.

Her father went back to fishing for a coffee cup. "It's

29

Saturday. Aren't you going to go exploring? I'll bet this town is full of kids your age."

Emma handed her father his muffin half. "I'm full up with friends, Daddy."

Leo Cake paused before taking a bite of muffin and said, "You can never have too many friends, Emma. Why, I've got friends from Kingdom to Come, and glad for every one of them."

He waved his muffin in the air for effect. "My friend Albert Stacks—best mechanic in three counties in Texas— was just on my mind this morning." He took a giant bite of muffin. *"Ummmmph. Goooood."*

Emma sighed. She couldn't remember the last time one of her father's friends had visited. But he seemed to be a happy man. She watched him eat the other muffin half. The radio played "I'm So Lonesome I Could Cry."

"It's a Hank Williams *bonanza!*" said her father. "Boy, that's an old song."

A little muffin, a little music, a little sleep, and he *was* a happy man. There was no arguing with him, either. Her life was what it was. She had better get used to it. Again.

Her thoughts returned to her Friend Atlas still rolled up in her suitcase. She wouldn't even unroll it this time.

She made up her mind. She would be sensible and practical.

No friends here. None. She wanted to be happy, too.

She would start now.

30

~ *Chapter Six* ~

Ben Cake didn't feel very Lord Baltimore anymore. After he had swept up the oats on Miss Mattie's wooden floor, she had him empty them into the compost she kept in a neat bin in the wide dirt alleyway between her store and the building that had been Doc MacRee's office and was now Ben's new home.

She also handed him a bucket of spent produce—kale, mostly . . . no one was buying the kale this week—from the refrigerator case. Into the compost it went. Then she'd made Ben water the compost, turn it with a pitchfork, and water it again.

"Well done," Miss Mattie said, hands on her shirtwaist dress and broad hips, as she surveyed Ben's handiwork. The gnats were fierce and the flies were biting.

"Thank you," Ben replied, because he didn't know what else to say. He looked with great longing at the baseball field.

"You show up here for a few hours on Wednesdays and Fridays, and you've got a job," said Miss Mattie. "I pay in cash, and you'll have spending money."

"But . . ." began Ben. He looked at Miss Mattie, his unhappiness plastered all over his face.

"No buts," said Miss Mattie. "Your mother approved it, and I need an extra set of hands. Those are our busiest days, aside from Saturdays when I have Eula's help. You'll be working with my great-niece, Ruby. You met her a bit ago."

Indeed he had, when Ruby had followed the Cake boys into the store after retrieving her notes from the silver maple. He could recall every word.

"Who are *you*?" Ruby had asked. Full stop. Ben had just stared back. *Nobody,* he'd wanted to say, but he hadn't said a word. *None of your business* also occurred to him, but he hadn't said that, either.

"That's my eldest, Ben," sparkled Arlouin Cake. "Benjamin Lord Baltimore Cake, meet Ruby Lavender. She's not very sweet."

"What a mouthful," said Miss Mattie, who had not accepted a muffin to eat, but did take several to put in a basket by the cash register. "Is that the name on his birth certificate?"

Arlouin nodded. "Absolutely! We named each of our children after the cake we were baking when they were born."

"Let me hear them." Miss Mattie crossed her arms in front of her chest. Each Cake boy spoke around the muffin he was eating and muffled out a name.

"Humph!" said Miss Mattie. "And I suppose you"—she

gave Arlouin a sharp look—"are the only family member without a cake name, since you married into the family."

"Oh no," said Arlouin quickly, happily. "I took my husband's name, Cake, when we married, and added Hummingbird Spice! We had a hummingbird spice wedding cake. Four layers tall. With Corinthian column support pillars!"

Miss Mattie pursed her lips as if she was trying to keep herself from making a remark she might later regret.

"We'll be opening the bakery just for experimental purposes for the next week or two . . . or more . . . while we work out the kinks," said Arlouin, as if she'd been asked about this. "The Grand Opening celebration will be a week or so after that. Our landlady, Miss Eula Dapplevine, has secured our permits and has been most generous about seeing that we have what we need to get started here in Halleluia."

Miss Mattie looked to the heavens, from whence her help did not come. "Why are you here?" she asked Arlouin.

"She's here because I rented them the building," said a voice from the front screen doors.

"Miss Eula!" Ruby forgot all about Benjamin Lord Baltimore Cake and ran to embrace her grandmother.

"It's been too long!" Miss Eula said, her granddaughter in her arms. "And no, that grandbaby Leilani is not cuter than you are, and Hawaii is not better than Halleluia, and

I told you I'd come back, and I did, just like last time. I left you a note already—did you get it?"

"I did," said Ruby, all smiles. "I didn't want to wake you up too early, because Mama said you'd be close to dawn getting in."

"Well, I'm here," said Miss Eula, as she looked beyond Ruby to the assemblage. "And it looks like everyone else arrived in good order as well."

"We did, indeed," said Arlouin Cake. "Thank you so much for all you did to make us comfortable last night."

"My pleasure," said Miss Eula. "My friend Tot brought the milk and butter and eggs. You can thank her when you meet her."

"If she brings food for a welcome gift, don't eat it," said Ruby.

Mary Wilson, Cleebo Wilson's mother, strutted purposefully through the front doors. "I'm all out of starch, Mattie," she said, "and we're about to open."

"This way," said Miss Mattie, glad for something concrete to do.

"Eula!" exclaimed Mary Wilson. "Glad to have you home. You missed quite a game yesterday. My Cleebo was a hero!"

"So I heard!" said Miss Eula. She turned to Arlouin. "You'll want to know Mary," she said. "She owns the Sunshine Laundry, three doors down, and she's your best bet for clean aprons, kitchen towels, tablecloths, and such."

Mary Wilson nodded at Arlouin as she followed Miss Mattie to the starch. "Pleasure to meet you," she called as she waved a hand, disappeared down an aisle, and broke into the Sunshine Laundry jingle: "Sunshine Laundry! Send us your sheets! Under new management! Can't be beat!"

Arlouin laughed. "I surely will," she called back.

Then she gathered her basket and her boys. "Cakes always know when to take their leave!"

"I'm not done with your boy," said Miss Mattie.

"Keep him for as long as you need him, anytime you need him!" chirped Arlouin.

And with that, she was gone, with Jody, Van, Roger, and Gordon trailing like obedient ducks behind her.

Ruby had run out with the boys, which had left Benjamin Lord Baltimore Cake inside with Miss Mattie, and now outside, standing beside a compost pile he'd just been congratulated on turning.

"Go get your glove," said Miss Mattie, as she followed Ben's gaze to the ball field where a gaggle of kids had gathered. "I expect you're done for today."

"Yes, ma'am!" Ben shouted, already halfway to the back door of the Mercantile.

"Hang up your apron!" she called after him. "Ask Eula if she needs any help first!"

Ben smiled to himself as he ran back inside the Mercantile, grabbed his glove from the counter and shoved it in his armpit, and waved at Miss Eula, who shooed him out the door. All things considered, he was doing well so far in this new place. He had a job! He had a ball field right next to his house, so there would always be baseball, no matter what else happened. *Next up,* he told himself: *Find a friend.*

∾ Chapter Seven ∾

All across Aurora County, at the same time Arlouin Cake was delivering her muffins and making friends (such as one can) with Miss Mattie Perkins, the children who had participated in the Aurora County 200th anniversary pageant and ball game against the Raleigh Redbugs the day before began to wake up. They yawned and stretched in their beds.

Cleebo Wilson, the All-Stars' first baseman, had stayed up late rereading the biography of Jackie Robinson his dad had given him long ago. "Met him once," he'd told Cleebo. "Had a catch with him while he was still in the Negro Leagues. I was just a kid."

Now that Cleebo knew that Pip, the eighty-eight-year-old hero of yesterday's All-Stars game, was his town's Jackie Robinson, he had a new appreciation for the man and his story.

Then there was Finesse, Pip's great-granddaughter, she of the theatrical black curls accented with blue tips. Finesse, with her bangling bracelets and her broken French. She woke up smiling as wide as the sun, ready to embrace her *biquettes*. Yesterday had been a hard-won triumph for her, getting the boys to agree to dance, the girls to play ball. Everyone together, *the symphony true*, she thought with a smug smile. House had taught her about the symphony true—it was part of a poem—and she remembered.

Melba Jane Latham woke up with her clipboard next to her bed, made a note in it that she thought Finesse would appreciate, and put on her second-best sundress and a pair of white lace gloves, even though it would be hot enough today to fry a round egg on a flat rock.

Honey, House's little sister, was already dressed in her shorts, shirt, and pink tutu. She ate a steaming plate of scrambled eggs that her father fixed for her. She spooned several bites into Eudora Welty's bowl. The old pug dog smacked her lips appreciatively. She wore a pink tutu as well.

Mr. Norwood Boyd's creaky, vine-covered house was through the woods on a path from Honey's house. It was empty now. Norwood had drawn his last breath earlier this summer, with House sitting next to him reading *Treasure Island*.

For years, Aurora County kids had claimed the house was haunted, had run quickly past it when they were on the county road, and had called Norwood Boyd terrible names behind his back, when none of them but House had even seen the man in all their lives. They hadn't understood.

But after yesterday's game, especially after Miss Mattie's speech, they knew differently.

Without planning it or saying a word to one another about it, the Aurora County All-Stars, ballplayers and dancers alike, began to show up at the baseball field behind Miss Mattie's store, in ones and twos and threes, like weary little ground balls that bump from home plate to the bases, most of the stuffing popped out of them.

Even House showed up. He wore his battered baseball cap and a sling that cradled his left elbow. They had won the game yesterday with House pitching for them, but he had destroyed his arm in the process. It hurt.

At the moment everyone arrived, Arlouin Cake emerged from Miss Mattie's store with a triumphant smile on her face. She was almost run over by Jody, Van, Roger, and Gordon. Ruby wasn't far behind, although she didn't run to the ball field. She sat on the back stoop of Miss Mattie's store and read her two notes.

"More kids!" shouted the Cake boys, although it sounded like *muff kuff,* as their mouths were full of muffins. They streaked across the sandy lane like the tail of one large comet minus their fiery nucleus, Ben.

"More kids," whispered Emma Lane Cake from her kitchen window outpost. Here were more kids in one place than she'd ever experienced on a first morning in a new home. Her brothers were accomplished at making a new friend before breakfast, but twelve new kids at once was a record.

"More kids?" asked Leo, who had finally found the

coffee cups. He opened the window over the kitchen sink to let in the breeze and the clangor, and took a long, appreciative sip of coffee he had drowned in sugar and milk. "This place is going to be a friend *bonanza*," he declared.

Emma thought of Annie, the friend she had just left, the friend who loved to braid Emma's hair. Annie looked like the tall, brown girl on the baseball field, with the blue-tipped hair clipped to the top of her head, who was so seriously poring over something on a clipboard that a girl with short buttery curls and a fancy dress was showing her.

Emma hadn't even put Annie in her Friend Atlas yet. She had cried for so long in the car after they'd left, she'd made herself sick somewhere in Arkansas. "We'll write," she and Annie had told each other, but Emma and her friends always said that and they never wrote.

It wasn't that they didn't want to be friends anymore. It's just that writing wasn't the same as being with someone. Writing required a remembrance of the pain of parting, for one thing. For another, life happened so fast and so much and so often, it was hard to even decide what to put on paper. Emma was better at drawing than writing, anyway.

The Aurora County kids were clustered under the chinaberry tree next to Halleluia School, which was on the far side of the ball field, when they spotted the Cake boys and dogs running for them.

"Hey!" shouted Evan Evans and Wilkie Collins.

"O mon père!" whispered Finesse.

Melba clasped her clipboard to her chest.

"Who is it?!" chirped Honey.

"Boy howdy!" cheered the Tolbert Twins, Ned and Boon.

George Latham, Melba's oldest little brother, screamed, "Score! Score! Score!"

And that was that. They took off running to meet their new friends halfway.

Jody, Van, Roger, and Gordon were right in the middle of the Aurora County kids now, a mess of dogs (theirs and others') barking around them. Jody and Van and their new buddies were happily pulling the Cake bicycles off the Ford Econoline. Wilkie Collins waved a bat and shouted for order. Evan Evans ran the bases, just for fun. Cleebo Wilson arrived, skidded his bicycle to a halt in the crowd, and almost ran over the Tolbert Twins, who threw their baseball gloves at him. "Score! Score! Score!" shouted little George Latham.

Melba wore her elegant white gloves and pointed to her important ideas on her clipboard. Eudora Welty plopped her ancient self in the morning shade near the schoolhouse, away from the Cake dogs and all the action. Van and Jody lobbed a ball back and forth and called for a pickup game, while Roger whined about his bike tires being flat, and Gordon watched Honey twirl in her tutu at home plate.

It was a glorious mess. *It's the dazzle of day,* thought House Jackson. He liked that line from Norwood Boyd's favorite poem in his favorite book by his favorite poet, Walt Whitman. House owned that book now. *The dazzle of day, the symphony true.* That's what it looked like to him.

House saw a new boy his age trotting over from Miss Mattie's store. He raised his good hand in greeting. "Hey," he said as Ben Cake got closer. Then he tugged on his baseball cap.

"Hey," Ben said back. No one needed to tell Ben that he would like this boy best. He already knew it.

Emma watched the messy glory from the upstairs kitchen and felt the tiniest tug on her heart. She shook her head. "I'm going to do the dishes," she told her father in a determined voice.

And that's when someone began pounding on the Cakes' back door downstairs.

"I know you're in there!" shouted Ruby Lavender. "Open up! I'm here for the soup!"

~ *Chapter Eight* ~

"Don't let her in!" cried Emma. "I've changed my mind!"

"About what?" Leo made his way downstairs. "We have to be neighborly," he insisted.

"I don't care about neighbors!" Emma shouted after him. "Please don't open the door!"

"We can't pretend we're not here!" her father called back. "Whoever it is knows we're in here!"

Leo opened the door. There she stood, Ruby Lavender, waving her note. Leo gave her a quizzical smile. His glasses slid down his nose. He invited her inside.

The four Cake dogs were ready for breakfast. An open door was an invitation. They pushed themselves in behind Ruby, *ga-bump, ga-bump, ga-bump, ga-BUMP,* before Leo could shut the door. As each dog galumphed past her, Ruby's body waved like a spindly sapling in the breeze. She struggled to keep from dropping her note and falling into Leo Cake. He stood with his arms out like he was trying to direct traffic.

"Whoa! It's rush hour at the Cakes'!"

When the dogs were past them and scrambling for the stairs, Ruby stood up straight, shoved her hair out of her face, and announced herself.

"Hi," she said, breathless. "I'm Ruby. Your dogs love me."

Leo Cake laughed. "And they know it's time to eat! Come on in! We'll feed you, too."

"No, thanks," said Ruby. "I'm here to meet your soup cooker."

"Ahh," said Leo. "That would be Emma."

"That's what your boys told me at Miss Mattie's store. You've sure got a lot of them."

"That we do," said Leo Cake.

Dishes crashed in the sink. Leo looked toward the stairs. "And we've got one beautiful girl."

Ruby pulled up her errant overalls strap. "I hope she's not too beautiful. We've got enough girls trying to be beautiful in this town."

Leo smiled at her and pushed up his glasses. "Emma!" he called up the stairs.

More crashing. The dogs whined for their breakfast. Or was it lunch?

Leo frowned. "Wait right here. I'll be back." He took the stairs two at a time.

Ruby heard a bag crunch and a cascading *ping ping! ping!!* into a metal bowl—several metal bowls—and dogs hungrily smacking their chops and growling warnings at one another and diving into their food. Someone turned up the radio. An old song about a buffalo herd sang out over the stairwell: "...*you can be happy if you've a mind to!*" Water ran. Pans clattered. Something crashed to the floor and broke. The dogs kept chomping. They were loud eaters.

And underneath the noise came the muffled sounds of a heated discussion. Ruby tiptoed up the stairs.

When she couldn't make out what they were saying in their strained, low voices, she peeped her head around the top of the stairwell. There stood the soup cooker. She had her back to the sink and was waving a wooden spoon at her father. He was sweeping up some broken glass. Packing boxes were everywhere.

The cook—*she must be Emma Lane Cake*—wore an apron that said I EAT PIE on it. Her face was on fire as she whispered fiercely, "I don't feel like it! Please!" The water filling the sink created a gigantic cloud of suds that began to cascade over the lip of the counter and onto the floor.

"Hey!" Ruby yelled, just as the splashing started. She leaped to the sink and turned off the water.

The tension evaporated. Leo, Emma, and Ruby stared at one another. The radio kept wailing. *"All ya gotta do is put your mind to it!"* The dogs kept chomping. Emma blinked at this red-haired girl in overalls—the one she had written to without knowing who she was.

To Whom It May Concern:

I am cooking an interesting soup Saturday afternoon. Please come.

Leo broke the standoff by dumping the pieces of glass from the dustpan into the trash and turning off the radio. "Ruby, this is Emma," he said. "Emma . . . meet Ruby."

"I don't want to meet Ruby," Emma said, her voice still full of that strained quality. She had thought it, but she was surprised she'd said it.

Ruby tried to think of what to say to that. She held Emma's note in front of her with two hands, close to her chest, like it was treasure. "I've got an *invitation*," she said with great ceremony, as if the paper's contents were a secret pact, written in blood. "I'm *To Whom It May Concern!*"

Leo Cake knew better than to try to get in the middle. "I'm going to help your mother with the shopping," he said. "We've got a bakery to get started." He slipped out of the kitchen.

Emma could see the determination on Ruby's face. But she was determined, too.

"I changed my mind," she told Ruby. But she couldn't take her eyes off this girl with freckles like hers and a lop-sided ponytail.

"Change it back!" popped Ruby.

"Nope." Emma stood up straight and held on to her promise to herself. "Sorry. No soup."

It was a stalemate. Neither giving in, neither looking away. So they looked each other in the face, resolute, for what felt like an ice age while they each wondered: *Now what?*

～ Chapter Nine ～

The sounds of a pickup baseball game drifted through the open kitchen window and Ruby couldn't help herself; she followed them. She looked at the field outside the window and back to Emma. Ruby was a good ballplayer, and she itched to bat against those new boys. But she decided to stay where she was.

The big black dog that Ruby thought resembled Comfort's dog, Dismay, began to lap at the water on the floor. Emma grabbed his water bowl. "Stop it, Bo-Bo!" she shouted. "That water's got soap in it! And there might be glass on the floor!"

"That's his name?" Ruby asked. "Bo-Bo?"

"Yes." Emma sighed as she let the water out of the sink and filled the dog's water bowl. "He's the dumbest dog ever born, so we just have to love him and hope for the best."

So much for any more resemblance to Dismay, who had been the most noble dog ever to draw a breath, in Ruby's opinion. Heck, in everybody's opinion in Aurora County.

"Who are the rest?" Ruby asked. She moved a box to the floor and situated herself on a kitchen chair. "I helped my fourth-grade teacher move into his house two years ago, and I could help you move into this one. I'm a good unpacker."

Emma shook her head. "We don't need help."

Bo-Bo gave Emma a sloppy, smelly kiss as she gave him his water. Emma pulled out a chair from the other side of the table and plopped down on it. She was going to have to talk to this girl, she could see.

A bat cracked in the distance and someone shouted, "You're out!" It was a new voice to Ruby, but she knew who it belonged to. It was that boy, Ben, whom she'd just met inside Miss Mattie's store. He might be friend material, too.

"Do you play baseball?"

Emma shook her head again. "I make soup. I help in the bakery."

"Oh." Ruby was unimpressed. But she didn't leave. Her friend Dove didn't play baseball, either, and Ruby didn't hold it against her.

A shaggy brown dog came to Emma for some love. "This one's Alice," Emma said. "We found her behind a Dumpster. Then she had Bo-Bo." Bo-Bo came back to Emma at the sound of his name and kissed her again.

"And that one is Spiffy." Emma pointed to an old red-and-brown dog—mostly a beagle, Ruby figured. He was still eating, and in a slow, methodical way. His belly was thick, his eyes drooped, his skin sagged, and his snout was white.

"He doesn't look spiffy," Ruby commented.

"He's not," said Emma. "Unless it's time to eat." She

smiled at Spiffy and he blinked at her when she called his name. He was her favorite.

The last of the four dogs, a long-legged, spotted blue-tick hound, laid its head in Ruby's lap. She scratched him behind his ears. "Who's this?"

"That's Hale-Bopp," said Emma.

"Hale-Bopp!" Ruby laughed. "Hello, Hale-Bopp." The dog shoved his snout under Ruby's hand, and ate her note in one big gulp. "Hey!"

"He does that," said Emma as the dog chewed on the paper. "Go get some water, Hale-Bopp." The dog loped over to the water bowl.

"Smart," said Ruby. Now she was impressed.

"Thirsty," said Emma. It was too easy, making this friend. It was like riding a bike—no matter how long it's been, you get on and you go. It was fun. She was doomed.

"I'm . . . I'm not going to make a soup today, after all," she said. "So you can go."

Ruby fidgeted in her chair. If there was one thing she loved, it was making a new friend, because the opportunity to do so was so rare. And because she was so *good* at it.

"Nobody new comes here anymore," Ruby said. "Everyone here is boring except my friend Dove, who really lives in Memphis and only comes for three weeks in the summer to visit her aunt and uncle—that's Mr. Ishee and his wife, Tot, the ones I helped move in two years ago."

Ruby used to tell Dove she talked too much, but Dove's habit had clearly rubbed off on Ruby. Now she gulped for air and breezed ahead. "Free advice: You'll be bored to tears here without me, you'll see. It'll be torture. You'll be stuck in this town with a beauty queen and a bad actress and a bunch of loony ballplayers, and when school starts next month, you won't have one friend you can count on. You *need* me!"

"I like being lonely," Emma said breezily. "Loneliness is a virtue."

Ruby hooted. "Is not!"

Despite herself, Emma laughed. She liked this girl. She could see she was going to make a friend whether she liked it or not. It was inevitable. She sighed a big, heavy sigh. Her poor heart. Her poor, poor heart.

Ruby watched the sadness slide across Emma's face. "Why did you change your mind about the soup?"

Emma stood up and walked to the window. She watched the boys playing ball, shouting and laughing, getting to know their new friends. She could change her mind again. Her best soup was a chicken noodle. But she didn't have any chicken.

As if on cue, a fat red hen scurried across the sandy lane and pecked at the ground under the silver maple tree. Emma took it as a sign.

"I think I *will* make soup!" she announced.

This friendship might work; she'd figure out the moving parts of it later. The impulsive note she'd left in the tree was inspired, and yes, this town *was* the one. *Yes.* All she had to do was believe it.

"Great!" said Ruby. "What kind?"

"Chicken!" crowed Emma. She pointed out the window to the silver maple and tried a joke, her first joke with her first new friend in this new forever town. "And there's one right down there! A stray chicken! Do you think we could catch it? My dad is good at wringing chicken necks, and chicken soup is my specialty!"

"What?" The word curdled in Ruby's throat. She shot from her chair so violently it fell backward and slapped the kitchen floor. In two giant leaps she was at the kitchen window, looking down at her errant chicken, Rosebud. *"Chicken soup?"* she managed to sputter as she pointed to her chicken.

"What?" Emma took a step away from her new almost-friend. She was alarmed. "What is it? Do you not like chicken soup?"

Ruby hadn't once considered she might not like this Emma Lane Cake. She didn't like Finesse, she tolerated Cleebo, she would never like Melba Jane, but she got along with most kids. She had been flattered to receive Emma's invitation. But she drew the line at killing chickens—*especially* her beloved Rosebud. Suddenly the room was airless, and she couldn't breathe. She had been about to befriend a *chicken murderer*, when she'd already saved her chickens from just such a fate.

"I have to go," she gasped. She thought she might vomit.

"Wait!" Emma said, her resolve completely melted now. "What's happening?"

Ruby stumbled her way over and around boxes and dogs. The dogs thundered and whirled down the steps with her. Ruby knew she should say something, but her mind wrinkled at the idea of murder. All that would come out of her mouth was a stray thought she'd had inside Miss Mattie's store earlier, so she hurled it at Emma in a murderous tone. "Your brother is cute!"

"What?" Now Emma was confused as well as alarmed. She ran after Ruby and stood at the top of the stairs.

Ruby chastised herself. *Your brother is cute?* She'd never thought a boy was cute. What was wrong with her? She needed to go hug her chickens. She yanked at the back door and out she flew, leaving the door wide open.

"What did I do?" Emma shouted after her. She stumbled over Spiffy and clattered down the stairs, to see what might come next.

∾ Chapter Ten ∾

By the time Ruby Lavender rushed out of Emma's house, everyone was outside but Miss Mattie and Miss Eula, who were busy with the first Saturday morning customers at the Mercantile. Somehow, there had been enough muffins for the hungry Cakes, enough for the dogs, enough for Miss Mattie's basket by the register, and now, enough to go around for the Aurora County All-Stars, ballplayers and dancers alike. It was as if Arlouin's muffin basket was bottomless. Maybe it was.

"I leave you to your ball game!" Arlouin trilled as she swanned over to the Ford Econoline, where Leo Cake had just finished unloading more boxes and was now waiting to go with his wife to Bay Springs, the next town over and the county seat, where there was a Piggly Wiggly for shopping. Their list was long and they were eager to get started.

"You boys take all these things inside when you're done!" he shouted to the Cake boys, and they waved their agreement.

That's when Ruby and the Cake dogs came rushing from the back of the Cakes' new home, with Emma on their heels.

"My land!" exclaimed Arlouin. "Where's the fire?"

"Emma and Ruby are becoming friends," explained her husband.

"That's a strange way to go about it!"

Leo Cake shrugged and opened the car door for his wife while saying in his most knowledgeable voice, "I do not pretend to understand the ways of women."

As Arlouin and Leo drove away, the Cake boys surrounded their sister. Emma bobbed her head to look between them, to see where Ruby had gone, but she couldn't find her.

Her brothers talked all at once. Of course. Gordon had made friends with Honey. He was wearing her tutu. It had been ridiculously easy. Jody—no angel—had beaned Cleebo with a line drive to second and only Cleebo's quick reaction with his glove had saved his life. Cleebo was recovering at Mr. Pip's barbershop, where—for some reason—there was an ice machine. House had walked over with him. He had business with Pip anyway, and also had an appointment with Doc MacRee for his elbow and said he'd take Cleebo and Ben with him. Van had soothed everyone's feelings with his chocolate-layer-cake voice, while Roger had whined, in his black-forest voice, that they were all going to be in big trouble when people found out Jody had smacked his line drive into Cleebo's head on purpose. Which Jody hadn't, Jody insisted. The game had fizzled from there.

But the game yesterday, her brothers told her, had been tremendous. They had missed it by just *hours*, but they would have another one next year, and her brothers would be sure to play in it.

We won't be here next year, Emma thought. *They always forget that. I forgot it just now, too.* She kept looking for Ruby in the crowd. She winced as she thought about her misdeed, and she didn't even know what she'd done.

Finesse stepped in front of Emma in all her glory and introduced herself—"*Bonjour, ma nouvelle amie!*"—and Emma thought of Annie, only Annie did not speak French. Still, it made her lower lip quiver and started an ache in her heart.

Melba Jane wrote Emma's full name on her clipboard: *Emma Alabama Lane Cake.*

"My goodness," Melba said.

"You might consider changing your name, like I did," said Finesse.

"She used to be Frances," Melba intoned.

"Now she's a shampoo!" volunteered Ned Tolbert.

"I like my name," said Emma. Because she did.

"Where are you from?" asked Melba Jane. "Your brothers didn't seem to know."

Emma thought of her Friend Atlas. "Everywhere and nowhere," she said. An answer that didn't satisfy, even as Melba Jane began to write it down on her paper.

Emma looked at this sea of potential new friends. None of them would break her heart to leave; she already knew that. There was only one she really wanted. Wasn't it always that way?

Gordon twirled to her and asked to be picked up. She obliged, tutu and all.

"Come here, Sticky Buns."

Again she looked for Ruby Lavender.

Ruby had disappeared.

THE AURORA COUNTY NEWS

HAPPENINGS IN HALLELUIA

special edition
compiled and reported by
Phoebe "Scoop" Tolbert

So much can happen in such a short time. That's what Mr. Tolbert always says, and he is always right. In this case, WE HAVE BAKED GOODS! Not that we lack for good cooks in Aurora County, but suddenly we have a bakery across the street from the Pine View Café, and Jerome Fountainbleu is beside himself with relief. "And there were *cakes*! And there were *pies*! And the prettiest *rolls* that you ever did see!"

It makes one want to belt out a chorus of "The Green Grass Grew All Around," doesn't it? Ahem. I digress. I have hosted my grandchildren from Pelahatchie this week, can you tell?

Doc MacRee moved out of his old digs and into the back half of the sheriff's department next to the barbershop owned by Parting Schotz (known colloquially, locally, as Pip). Personally, I would rather have seen Doc move into the back room of the barbershop, so as not to be tending to our little ones with chicken pox right next to our hardened criminals in the jail cells. Admittedly, we have never known a hardened criminal (or even a softened one) in Aurora County. The jail cells are full of hay right now.

The baked goods are coming from our new neighbors in Doc MacRee's old space! The Cake Family has been in residence for two weeks now. Or is it three? Where they came from, no one seems to know. And believe me, dear reader—you know me—I have asked.

Walking into the Cake Café (and Bakery) (as it is called) is an olfactory delight. The aromas! There is a massive commercial kitchen in the back—it seems to have appeared out of nowhere!—and glass cases out front full of the prettiest little rolls (and cookies and muffins and toast points and corn cakes) that you ever did see. And cakes! Of course. There are old wooden tables set with pretty flowers from

Evelyn Lavender's garden that add to the ambience. The scintillating scent of a good soup fills the air along with the floury goodness on display.

"Our business at the Pine View has tripled!" crowed Jerome Fountainbleu. "Customers must be coming from the state capital!"

They are not.

It is true that business is on the uptick at the Pine View, and that there are few extra citizens in Aurora County to justify the numbers. But where are these Cakes from? And—it must be asked—when they open to the public, will they pull business away from the Pine View, with their daily soup-and-sandwich offering and curated baked goods? I can envision whisking into the Cake Café to partake of a quick lunch of soup and bread, so unlike the slow-as-molasses meal service (it must be acknowledged) at the Pine View.

Plus, at the Cake Café (I have studiously discerned) there are two parents, four dogs, five boys, and one intrepid slip of a girl always working in the back whom I cannot wait to interview. You will also want to know that my keen eye has spotted none other than Misanthrope Watkins, former baker at the Pine View, in the Cake kitchen with a rolling pin in hand.

Stay tuned for more intrigue as I uncover it!

Yours faithfully, PT

∾ Chapter Eleven ∾

Emma was weary. It takes so much work to open a bakery, and she had been at it for at least two weeks—or was it three?—toting and chopping and stirring and beating and folding and scrubbing and wondering what she had done to lose a friend before she'd even had one.

There had been no time to find Ruby and ask. And she had talked herself into being fine with that. So why did she keep thinking about it?

"Because it makes me angry!" she growled as she buttered muffin tins by herself in the kitchen. Why would that pushy girl suddenly turn on her and screech about her chicken soup and yell *I have to go* with no explanation and then run off shouting, *Your brother is cute*?

Emma wanted to yell at her. *You should apologize to me! What's wrong with you?!* On the other hand, Emma never wanted to see this girl again.

And she was busy.

"Cakes know when it's time for All-Cakes-on-Deck!" called her mother every day when it was time to work together.

Her brothers were good workers. As long as they were allowed an hour of riotous behavior every two hours, they were the hardest workers she knew. Even Gordon was a good helper. He washed baseboards and thresholds with a bucket of soapy water and a toothbrush, and kept calling everyone to look at his handiwork as the water got dirtier, until Emma changed it for him and brought him a new bucketful.

Everything they needed had appeared, just as it always did. Ovens, sinks, prep tables, refrigerators, racks, carts, cake pans, muffin tins, cookie sheets, fans, bakery cases, tables, chairs, cushions for the chairs, even the sweet little vases for the old wooden tables.

While the Cakes worked, town folks stopped in, in that polite and nosy way people did, to say welcome and to see what was happening. Arlouin and Leo gave them samples of whatever was coming out of the ovens. Cinnamon rolls, coffee cakes, cupcakes, pecan chewies, almond bars, sourdough bread, cheesecake, carrot cake, pineapple upside-down cake, cake-cake-cake. The Cakes were using this setup time to test their ovens and establish their kitchen flow and routines in a new space. And to see what their future customers liked best. The best smells in town were coming from the Cake Café.

Some, like Agnes Fellows, were suspicious of new people, and full of questions. "Is there some reason we need another café in town?"

Some, like Harvey Popham, were worried about any change in their small town. "Next, I suppose we'll have two banks, or two doctors—where will it end?"

Jerome Fountainbleu stopped in several times, to try the red velvet cake or the dark chocolate bear claws and thank the Cakes for supplying his pies. But as week one turned into week two, his thanks got less effusive and his visits were fewer. Suddenly he wasn't sure the town needed two cafés, either.

Dot Land, the postmistress, came by daily for a bite of something—"for my husband, Anton!" she always said. Dot loved cake and was quite sure the town needed two cafés.

So was Mary Wilson, who stopped in at lunch every day to sample Emma's latest soup. The corn chowder was her favorite. This thrilled Emma—a regular customer for her soups already.

The Aurora County kids stopped in, too, and some of them even picked up a broom or helped organize the kitchen with the boys (making a colossal mess that Emma and her mother had to undo).

But Ruby hadn't come, not even when her grandmother, Miss Eula, stopped by to check on her renters and bring flowers from her daughter Evelyn's garden. Evelyn Lavender was the county extension agent, and Ruby was her only child—Emma had discovered that by scrubbing hard and listening carefully.

So the Cake Café was the talk of Halleluia. Folks were used to coming in the back door to visit Doc MacRee, so that's where they all showed up, but the back of the building now opened into the mammoth kitchen, so it was reserved for family comings and goings, and deliveries. After folks tried the back door, they figured it out and came to the front.

Finesse came through the front door now, stumbling over Gordon, and followed by Spiffy, Alice, Bo-Bo, Hale-Bopp . . . and Melba Jane, who tried not to touch the dogs. That was impossible. The dogs *loved* Melba Jane, and Melba Jane hated slobber. She stood on a chair with her clipboard and hissed at the dogs until they quit loving her.

"*Bonjour, ma nouvelle amie!*" said Finesse.

Emma was fitting little bunches of Evelyn Lavender's flowers into the vases on each café table. She blinked. "Hi."

Finesse steamed ahead. "*Mon oncle,* who plays Dr. Dan Deavers on the television show *Each Life Daily Turns, and* who was our stellar umpire for our All-Stars game and pageant earlier this month, *and* who supplied our stage, all the way from Los Angeles, is about to come out of his coma on the television show, so is going back to California. Would you like to come to a going-away party—a *soirée*—in his honor?"

Emma would not. But standing next to Finesse felt like being next to Annie, so in a moment of weakness she said yes.

"We're calling it the Dr. Dan Deavers Going-Away Soiree!" warbled Finesse.

"Perfect!" said Arlouin from her perch on a ladder, where

she was washing the huge front windows. Emma couldn't see her mother's face, but she knew she was smiling.

Then, "Hello!" Arlouin cried. She waved across the street at Jerome Fountainbleu, who was clearing off a table for customers at the Pine View. Jerome spotted Arlouin on her ladder and waved back, although not as enthusiastically as he had waved the day before and the day before that. And the day before that.

Melba Jane, wearing a bright-yellow sundress and yellow gloves, marked on her clipboard that Emma would be present at the soiree. "Across the street, at Mr. Pip's barbershop," she told Emma as she towered above her, the dogs on the floor surrounding her chair. "Tomorrow afternoon at four o'clock. Sharp. Dress is soiree casual."

"*Très bien!*" chirped Finesse. "Very good, *mon petit chou!*"

"You keep calling me that," said Melba, uncertain.

"It's a term of endearment," Finesse assured Melba Jane. "Because you are dear to me. I will miss you when I go back to the Lanyard School in August."

Miss Mattie blew through the front screen door. It slapped behind her. She was still furious with Miss Eula for not giving her the extra storage space, but she finally couldn't help herself and had to see what was happening next door.

"Mattie!" cried Arlouin Cake. "What a nice surprise!" She slowly climbed off her ladder, talking the entire time. "We are open to everyone for experimentation for as long as it takes us to work out the kinks and find our rhythm here. Just drop in whenever and help us sample and taste and tweak! Doesn't it smell divine in here! Grand Opening is next week! Or so! Welcome!"

"I tried to get in the back, like I used to," shot Miss Mattie, shooing away Bo-Bo, who had come to kiss her. "You've got an entire commercial kitchen back there now!"

"We do," said a smiling Leo Cake, who emerged from the kitchen and stood near the glass case by the wooden tables. He wiped his hands with his white chef's apron. Flour dusted his forehead and speckled his glasses. Behind him, in the kitchen, Jody, Van, and Roger were crashing the dishes. Some would call it washing.

"How much can you fit in that Ford Econoline?" Miss Mattie asked, hands on her hips and head cocked like an accusation.

"It's bigger inside than it looks!" Leo Cake answered.

"What made you choose to come here, of all places?" asked Miss Mattie. Her eyes narrowed.

Arlouin handed her a mop. "Life is full of mysteries," she said in a bright voice. "Want to help us get ready to open?"

"I do not!" said Miss Mattie, handing the mop right back. "I have customers! Ruby is over there by herself!"

Ruby! Emma's heart quickened and then sank.

"I came to fetch Ben," said Miss Mattie. "He is three minutes late for his shift. If I have to fetch him, what good is he to me?"

Ben came out of the kitchen wearing hot mitts and carrying a gigantic tray of cookies. They smelled like chocolate and brown sugar and cream and butter and maybe even chocolate chips. Yes, chocolate chips. They were like little cakes. Of course.

"I just pulled these out of the oven," Ben said, as explanation for his tardiness.

Arlouin beamed at Miss Mattie. "Want a cookie? These are called When You're So Tired You Can Hardly See Straight Cookies. We will serve them at our Grand Opening! I hope you'll come help us celebrate!"

Miss Mattie harrumphed and started for the back door, then abruptly wheeled and stomped to the front door and out she went. Spiffy, Alice, Bo-Bo, and Hale-Bopp galumphed after her, one-two-three-four, their nails clicking on the wooden floor and scrabbling over Gordon's clean threshold.

"For pity's sake!" Miss Mattie cried. Her voice faded as she got farther away, but she kept on admonishing the dogs who would try to follow her right into the Mercantile.

Arlouin sighed. "Cakes always know when to rest," she said. "Let's cool off. Let's have a cookie." She turned on the big overhead fan, reached for the cookie her son handed her, and sat with a weary thud at one of the tables Emma had decorated. "Thank you, Benjamin Lord Baltimore Cake. *Yum.*"

"Break time!" yelled Leo Cake to the boys in the kitchen. The crashing and the cascading sound of rushing water stopped. Jody and Van argued themselves to the front of the store, with Roger whining right behind them.

Everyone had a seat. Finesse had a cookie. Melba had a cookie. Gordon had two. They really were extraordinary cookies. Jody, Van, and Roger each had three. The only sounds for a few minutes were chewing and swallowing. Very companionable sounds. Leo brought in some cold lemonade and poured everyone a tall glass. Melba even removed her gloves.

"It's like a Parisian café!" Finesse whispered. *"Formidable!"*

For a moment life felt absolutely perfectly perfect to Emma. The perfect summer day. Hot and cookied, with hard work and lemonade. And . . . friends?

She had been invited to a party, after all. And she had said yes. And these friends wouldn't break her heart. They would be more like acquaintances. That was the way to go. Why hadn't she realized this seven moves ago?

Ben waved a hand to his mother. "Got to go to work."

Jody, Van, and Roger groaned together. "It's time for a pickup game! House and Cleebo and Wilkie and Evan and the Tolbert Twins are coming! And more! We need you!"

"Start without me," Ben told them. "I'll be there."

"Is Honey coming?" asked Gordon. His voice was full of helpless hope.

"Probably so," whined Roger. "You two have to stay off the bases today." Gordon beamed. He didn't care about the bases. But he had put a tutu on his Christmas list, even though it was only July.

Abruptly, Finesse made her thanks to the Cakes—"*Merci beaucoup!*"—and Melba pulled on her gloves. Finesse eyed Ben. "We're heading next door, too, as a matter of fact," she cooed. She had been trying to charm Ben for weeks, finding an excuse to visit the Cake Café every day, or to visit at Miss Mattie's when Ben was working.

Ben blushed and shrugged, his usual response when confronted with Finesse, or any girl. Wait. There had never *been* a girl to worry about before. This was torture. He grabbed his baseball glove, shoved it into his armpit, and double-timed it to the door.

Emma popped up from her seat. "Wait!" *Another impulsive decision*, her practical mind began. But then she pushed the thought away. She would do it.

"What?" asked her brother.

"I'm coming with you," she said.

∽ Chapter Twelve ∽

Miss Mattie's store was thick with customers on this sweltering July afternoon. Spiffy, Bo-Bo, Alice, and Hale-Bopp lifted their heads from the sidewalk and thumped their tails at Emma as she trailed the gaggle of kids through the front door of the Mercantile.

The dogs were hot and ready for a nap under the store's shady canopy. Arlouin Cake, who knew a thing or two about her daughter, had pressed some coins into Emma's palm as she left the café. "Buy us a Co-Cola for later," she whispered with a smile.

This was good. It gave Emma a concrete reason for going next door.

The cold-drink case was at the back of the store, which meant Emma had to thread herself through the folks buying work shoes and sun hats and dusting powder and tins of sardines or tuna. It was easy to lose her new acquaintances, who were already busy canvassing the customers about the soiree. Melba scribbled furiously on her clipboard.

Miss Mattie tied a starched bib apron—fresh from the Sunshine Laundry—on Ben, who was used to aprons, but grimaced at being trussed into one so unceremoniously, like he was Gordon's age and needed help.

"I know how to put on an apron," he complained to Miss Mattie, loud enough for onlookers to hear.

"When you're on time, you can fasten it yourself," Miss Mattie sniffed, also loud enough for anyone close to hear. Ben's face reddened. He and Emma exchanged a look as Emma walked past her brother. Emma shrugged. Ben raised an eyebrow back.

Then his eyes fell on Ruby working behind the counter and he shrugged at her. Ruby gave Ben a disinterested look, then worried that he might misinterpret it to mean *I think you're cute!*—this was torture—so she shifted into her most athletic voice and said, "I'm playing ball after my shift," to which Ben replied, "Me too."

"You can make up your three minutes on the other end," said Miss Mattie. She swatted Ben's shoulder in a that's-that way as she finished tying his apron. "Go. Mrs. Watson needs five pounds of butter from the back. For what, heaven knows. We're out of brooms. Bring three more out to the front."

Ruby had a paper sack full of groceries in her arms. She was wearing the exact same thing she'd worn a week ago when she and Emma had met: overalls, a faded red-striped shirt, and her hair in a sloppy ponytail.

She was probably wearing flip-flops, too, thought Emma. She noticed a huge pile of them spilling out of a box near the cold-drink case. What was it with the flip-flops? She got her drink and got in line with the other customers.

"Hey there, young lady!" said a man wearing a panama hat.

"It's nice to see the young folks," said another. "Even if they're strangers!"

"Yessirree," agreed yet another. "I believe you're from next door!"

Emma smiled and nodded. "Yessir," she said. "I'm Emma."

"What a nice name!" said a woman who smelled of lilacs. Then she added, "We already have a café, across the street!"

"She's from the new café!" said the man in the panama hat. "I know all about it." But he didn't, of course.

They all waited for Emma to tell them all about it, but she wasn't sure what to say. Spontaneity wasn't her gift. She could have said, *We're kind of open for business while we work out the kinks, and our cakes are wonderful— the soup is even better—and our Grand Opening celebration is in the next week—or so—please come!* She might have said, *Yes, another café, we know, but there must be a good reason for it, or we wouldn't have come!* But chitchatting wasn't her way.

It *was* Ruby's way, however. Ruby handed a paper sack to a customer across the counter. "Thank you so much, Mrs. Evans," she said. "I hope the baby is over his diarrhea. Please come again soon."

"Goodness!" said Mrs. Evans as she hastily made for the door.

Ruby's eyes fell on Emma, who was two customers back in line, but she didn't acknowledge her. Emma straightened her shoulders against the snub and listened to the other customers in line move on to gossip about their neighbors. And the café. And even about the pies at the Pine View.

In line two people in front of Emma, Goldie Shuggars slid a pound of sugar across the counter to Ruby and said, "Good morning, Ruby, this will be all today. Comfort and I are still trying to perfect Great-great Aunt Florentine's brownies!"

"Good morning, Miz Shuggars," said Ruby as she made change for the sugar and bagged it. "Tell Comfort hey from me. Tell her I saw her write-up about Ornette Coleman in the paper. There were three typos!"

"I'll do that!" said Goldie as she left the line.

Miss Mattie began to ring up Mrs. Varnado's order and Ruby bagged it. Emma was next in line. She could feel the heat from Ruby's anger. She was so uncomfortable she almost lost her nerve. She kept her eyes on the soda in her hand and concentrated on how familiar it would feel to split the sweet drink at the end of the day, pour it over vanilla ice cream in two glasses, and sit with her mother, planning the next day's baking. Or soup. Or both. Like they'd done a hundred times. It was their ritual. Safe. Comforting.

Her thoughts were interrupted by a crisp Miss Mattie. "Will that be all, young lady?"

"Yes, ma'am," Emma answered, startled into the present moment. She put her coins on the counter and looked straight at Ruby. Now that she was here, what would she say? She summoned her courage and opened her mouth.

"Hi" was all that came out.

Ruby didn't say a word. She shoved the drink at Emma. She didn't bother to bag it. She didn't say, *Thank you, come again soon.* Her look meant, *Come again never.*

Even though the line was long behind her, and Miss Mattie was nothing if not efficient, Emma lingered at the counter and stared into Ruby's heated gaze. Another completely impractical feeling passed through her and she suddenly knew she could not waste this opportunity. What good was a breathing tree and a talking breeze if you didn't honor them?

"We never stay anywhere long," she started, in a firm voice that was also as quiet as she could make it because it was not meant for those in the line behind her, but of course everyone who was close enough was all ears. "I always have to leave my friends, but you are the first friend who ever left me, before we even got started." Ruby blinked and Emma finished. "I didn't mean any harm."

Emma steeled herself for one more moment to see if Ruby would answer, but Ruby pursed her lips and glared harder.

Fine, thought Emma as her impractical feeling vanished. *I misunderstood. Forget the tree and the breeze and the night that felt like magic.* Emma's face burned with embarrassment. In front of all these people.

In one slow and deliberate move, Emma Lane Cake picked up her drink and walked out of Miss Mattie's Mercantile.

She did not look back.

～ Chapter Thirteen ～

In July the Mississippi nights are as hot as the days. The sun goes down past bedtime and the cicadas begin their nightly mating calls—some would call them screams—as soon as the soft dark begins to envelop the land.

Emma and her mother sat outside behind the bakery on lawn chairs, beside the sandy lane, with their ice-cream floats, facing the ball fields. The usual havoc was going on around the bases. "Score! Score! Score!" little George Latham kept calling.

"So we're open for business all this coming week, again informally, while we work out the kinks," said Arlouin. "And the Grand Opening celebration will be next week. Or so."

"Got it," said Emma. Her heart wasn't in it.

"You okay?" asked her mother.

"I'm fine," Emma replied. Then she changed the subject. "How can those boys even see?" On the ball field her brothers and the All-Stars were thick into their game. Ruby wasn't with them, and neither were Finesse or Melba or any of the dancers from the pageant. The spell that had brought them all to the ball field together on the Cakes' magical first day in Halleluia was finally dissipating. But those who loved the game would remain forever.

Honey and Gordon sprawled beside the third-base line, lying on their stomachs and coloring, with five dogs surrounding them: Spiffy, Alice, Bo-Bo, Hale-Bopp, and Eudora Welty. Eudora snored loudly as a wooden bat hit a wide pitch thrown by Cleebo Wilson and shouts erupted from the clutch of boys.

"That ball was a no-see-um!" yelled Jody as an excuse for why he missed Ned Tolbert's pop fly into center field.

"Let's wrap it in Day-Glo tape!" shouted Cleebo. "We've got some at the laundry!"

"Laundry's closed!" hollered Boon Tolbert.

"Time to call it a day," House Jackson said. He couldn't play anyway, with his bum elbow. He adjusted his baseball cap. "I've got to get Honey home."

"Aw, rats!" cried Gordon.

"I can't see what I'm coloring anyhow," said Honey. "See you at the sore-bay tomorrow, Gordon. Dress up!"

"Soiree," corrected Ben.

"Sore-bay," repeated Honey. She patted on her dog. "C'mon, YouDoggie!"

Eudora snorted awake and struggled to her feet.

"Mom, I'm going over to House's for a few," shouted Ben, and when Arlouin didn't protest, Ben dissolved into the shadows near the schoolhouse with Honey and House and Eudora.

The rest of the Cake boys didn't protest their brother's decision. They wandered off the field as one large, lost

77

amoeba, pushing a little, complaining a lot, tired and dusty and ready for showers and bed.

"One game of Parcheesi," offered Jody. He scooped up Gordon and whistled for the dogs.

"It takes too long," argued Van.

"You always cheat!" whined Roger.

"You can't count!" Jody complained.

Boys and dogs squabbled past Emma and their mother without saying a word to them. Maybe they didn't see them. They clattered across the threshold of their bakery home yelling, "Dad!" and the red door slammed shut. Their absence created a vacuum that the cicadas began to fill with their songs.

"Thanks for buying the Co-Cola," said Arlouin. "How was business in Miss Mattie's store?"

"Brisk," said Emma.

"Good. Maybe that means we'll have a good crowd in the café this week, which will bring us a nice fat crowd for the Grand Opening. Did people ask about us?"

"People wondered why we were opening a café when there was one across the street already."

Arlouin sighed and didn't comment. After a pause, she said, "Gonna be a handsome moon tonight."

Emma lifted her face to the last of the light in the sky. Then she looked from the Ford Econoline to the knothole in the silver maple. Even if there had been a note in it, it would not have been for her. The embarrassment fevered her face again as she remembered the scene at Miss Mattie's store. She slapped at a mosquito. "Time to go in," she said.

"So we're decided," said Arlouin. "No scones tomorrow, a luscious carrot cake, and yes to chicken soup. I'd like to hand out samples of everything, to get folks excited for the Grand Opening. Chicken soup is your specialty, you know."

"I know," said Emma, without enthusiasm.

Arlouin changed the subject. "I see you hung your Friend Atlas."

Emma sighed. "I did." She hadn't been able to resist doing it, after she'd walked out of Miss Mattie's store. She needed to be with her friends. She'd unrolled the atlas and cried. A cloud moved away from the sun at that moment and the low afternoon light spilled into Emma's room. It seemed to whisper, *Over here . . . on this wall . . . I will shine on your very true friends . . . friends who would never embarrass you . . . and I'll bring you love and best wishes from them at the end of every day.* It was a comfort.

And so she had hung her atlas. She stared at it for a long time. Remembering. And yet, even with the Friend Atlas, some memories were becoming hazy. She hated that.

She still needed to add Annie to the atlas. So she spent the hour before supper drawing her friend from memory and affixing the sketch to her atlas. She would add details later. Both of their addresses, the map from Emma's house to Annie's house, the time Emma had learned to cornrow Annie's hair and Annie had learned to French braid Emma's, the fact that Annie was a faster runner than Emma but Emma was a better climber than Annie, and how saying the word *petunias* would send them both into fits of laughter. It became their secret password. She would keep working on these things as she had time.

Now, outside in the gloaming, Arlouin gave Emma's arm two pats. "I've left friends, too."

Emma gave her mother a doleful look, close to tears, and Arlouin gave her daughter an understanding smile. "Do you remember Franny Chapman's mother?"

Emma shook her head. She didn't even remember Franny Chapman.

"Well, maybe it was before your time," said her mother. "Or maybe you were too little to remember. Anyway, she was my best friend about eight moves ago. I still miss her. Her name was Nadine. We went bowling together on Tuesdays. In a bowling league!"

Emma stared out at the empty ball field. Mother and daughter sat together, each lost in her own thoughts. A mockingbird began to sing with confidence from high in the silver maple tree.

"It's trying to imitate a Carolina Wren," said Arlouin. She smiled.

As Emma listened, a lumpy, shadowy figure came into view, walking on the sandy lane from the direction of the Sunshine Laundry.

Arlouin's eyes narrowed. "Who is that? I need your father's glasses!"

Emma squinted in the direction of the lump. It was short. Soon, Emma could see it was a girl. In overalls. Wearing flip-flops. Carrying a chicken.

Emma swallowed. "That's Ruby Lavender," she said, as the lump was almost upon them.

Arlouin sighed. "She's not very sweet."

"She's not sweet at all," said Emma.

"I heard that!" called Ruby.

Chapter Fourteen

Ruby stopped in front of Emma and her mother. The chicken filled Ruby's arms. She looked to be asleep. Emma judged it to be the same chicken she'd seen out the window.

"Hunting for chickens, dear?" asked Arlouin with a half smile.

"This one is mine," said Ruby. "I just came to introduce her to Emma. To show her that she wasn't an eating chicken."

"It looks like she eats plenty," noted Arlouin.

"I mean, she's not a chicken you eat," said Ruby, trying to be clear.

Arlouin stood up and gathered the glasses. "I am going to supervise showers," she said, "or none will be taken. Then I am getting a long, sweet soak after this long, hot day." She gestured to Ruby to take her folding chair. "I will make friends with chickens you don't eat another day, dear."

As the cicadas' chorus softened, Emma could hear the crickets' insistent serenade. She heard one fat bullfrog from the mudhole near the outfield—the same mudhole she'd pulled Gordon out of, tutu and all, earlier. And was that an owl calling from the tall pines at the other side of the ball field? Already? The birds had barely gone to sleep. The night world was coming awake.

Ruby didn't sit down. "This is Rosebud," she said. "She used to be small enough to fit in my front overalls pocket. I took her everywhere then. Miss Eula and I rescued her mother and two more hens from certain death when Peterson's Egg Ranch closed two years ago and they sent all the hens away to be chicken for your chicken soup."

Emma slapped at another mosquito. She said nothing. What was there to say? *Hi, Rosebud? Sorry your girl is so mean?*

The hefty Rosebud opened one round eye and looked at Emma, like she was waiting for a reply, then closed it.

Ruby spoke again. "That's why when you wanted to wring her neck it upset me."

Emma mustered her most sarcastic tone. "*I* wasn't upset at *all*."

Ruby ignored Emma's remark. "I don't eat meat," she said. "Neither does my grandmother, Miss Eula."

"Well, I do," replied Emma. "Why should you care?"

"I don't care if other people eat chicken," said Ruby. "I just don't want them to eat *mine*."

Emma sighed. "It was *a joke*."

"I can't joke about my chickens."

"No kidding." Emma stood up and slapped at a last mosquito. "I'm getting eaten up out here. I've got to go."

"Hey. I'm trying to tell you I'm sorry," said Ruby. "You don't know how rare that is! You should be impressed!"

"You didn't seem sorry at all this afternoon at Miss Mattie's store!" Emma shot back.

"I'm sorry for that, too," Ruby said quickly.

"Do you know how embarrassing that was for me?"

"You surprised me!"

"I stood in line for ten minutes! Long enough for you to stop being surprised!"

"No," said Ruby. "What you said. That's what surprised me. Didn't you see me blink? I blink when I don't know what to say."

"And you glare."

"Okay, I glare. I was still mad. Now I'm not."

Emma raised her eyebrows and gave a long look to the girl who might have been her friend. She didn't see the point in arguing. She said nothing.

Ruby put Rosebud down. The chicken shook herself awake and trotted to the base of the silver maple, where she began to scratch in the dirt and make little staccato sounds, *tuck-tuck-tuck-tuck-tuck*.

Rosebud was cute. And portly. Emma couldn't imagine her fitting into Ruby's pocket. But she shook her head. She would not be dissuaded.

"Thank you for the apology," she said in a decisive voice, "but you're not my type of friend."

"What *is* your type of friend?" Ruby asked, a distressed edge in her voice.

"Oh, I don't know," said Emma, frustrated that Ruby would not let this go. "Loyal, faithful, hard-working."

"I'm all those things!" gushed Ruby. She waved her arms for effect.

"Honest," Emma continued.

"That, too! Ask anybody!"

"Calm."

"Okay, okay," said Ruby. "I'm not calm. But I *am* honest. Always. And all those other things! Just ask Miss Eula. She'll tell you the truth of it."

Then they were silent until another thought occurred to Ruby, an honest one, and she voiced it. "Miss Eula says I can be an acquired taste, but so is she, and that's a good thing. We just have to find the people who appreciate how wonderful we are."

Emma laughed, again in spite of her resolve. Wonderful, Ruby was not. She was pushy, where Emma was considered. She was explosive, where Emma was careful. She was irrational, where Emma was practical. Not a good match.

Rosebud scratched for bugs, but her heart wasn't in it. She made sleepy cooing sounds and flopped onto her bottom, on a root, tucking her feet under her.

"She really wants to go to sleep," said Ruby. "It's past her bedtime."

"Mine, too," said Emma. She stood up with great speed, a final decision made. "I'm sorry, Ruby. It won't work." She headed for the back door of her house.

"Wait!" Ruby raced ahead of Emma and plastered herself, like a giant squid, against the tall red door, arms and legs outstretched. "Wait!"

"I have work to do," said Emma, even though she was impressed. She would go upstairs and work on her Friend Atlas and fill out index cards about Annie, a true friend, a perfect friend, a friend who would never embarrass her on purpose.

But Ruby would not move and Emma did not know how to peel her off the door. This crazy girl was chasing after her, insisting and insulting at the same time. Emma had no map for this kind of friendship.

Ruby could sense Emma's hesitation. "Want to see the greenhouse where my chickens live?" she offered. Without moving.

Emma tore her eyes off Ruby and concentrated on the milk-box cooler on the stoop, the one that had held the butter and eggs and milk the night they'd arrived, the night she'd first spied the note in the tree and had written one herself, back when she had believed for a few minutes that all things were possible and had longed her heart out for a friend. A sane friend, it occurred to her now.

Ruby fretted. "It won't take long. Do you want to see it?"

The edges of Emma's resolve began to fray. She looked at Ruby again. The longing for a friend was written all over Ruby's face, and Emma understood that longing so well. It spoke to her.

Emma lifted her head to the wide night sky and sighed. "Yes," she said. Of course she did.

~ Chapter Fifteen ~

Just like that, Emma was lost. She was hopelessly, help-lessly, happily lost in a new friendship. She gave herself to it completely. Suddenly she knew everything about her new friend, because Ruby told her every story she could cram into the short walk from Emma's to Miss Eula's house.

She heard the story about the daring chicken rescue, two years ago, of Ivy, Bemmie, and Bess. She heard about the old war between Ruby and Melba and how Melba had thrown a brick at the greenhouse one night, had shattered a window, and how two of Ivy's chicks had died before they were born. Rosebud was the one who had lived. No wonder Ruby was so attached to her.

She heard about Melba's blue hair accident, and Mrs. Varnado's fear of chickens and Aunt Tot's terrible cook-ing and Ruby's baseball career and her fights with Cleebo, and her arguments with Miss Mattie, and her disagree-ments with Miss Eula, who had first left her two years ago to go to Hawaii to see a new grandbaby—Ruby called her Hortense—and how Miss Eula finally came back with four hundred pairs of flip-flops to sell in Miss Mattie's store.

"I'm sure you fight with a lot of people," said Emma in a matter-of-fact voice.

"I don't fight!" Ruby protested. "I *discuss*."

"I have seen how you discuss," said Emma.

By the time they reached Miss Eula's house, the Pink Palace, Ruby was running out of stories. And that was fine, because the walk in the darkness had worked its magic on Emma. As the two friends came to Miss Eula's house, Emma put up a hand and said, "Shhh!"

"Isn't it great?" asked Ruby, pride in her voice. "Miss Eula and I painted it ourselves after Grandpa Garnet died." Even in the moonlight, the Pink Palace was very . . . pink.

"Shhh!" Emma repeated. She felt something familiar.

She had had her doubts about listening to a talking tree or a chatty breeze or even her own good heart, but now, walking through the rich warm night with its enchanted sights and sounds and smells, she wanted to believe.

In a way she couldn't articulate, this town knew her. Every living thing was alive and calling to her. She would ask her father again to remember.

They let themselves into the backyard through the garden gate. Black-eyed Susans grew along the fence and by the greenhouse. Emma reached out to touch them. She felt them reach out to her in kind.

"They were my grandfather's favorite," Ruby said as she picked one and handed it to Emma, which brought Emma back into the moment with Ruby.

Rosebud sprinted to the greenhouse. Ruby opened the door for her. "C'mon," she whispered to Emma as she waved her inside. "Just a peek."

A jasmine vine grew on an old bean trellis nearby, and the night air was sweet. Stars began to twinkle high in the sky as Emma stepped into the greenhouse. The floor was strewn with fresh pine shavings. Eight chickens crowded together on their wide ladder-like roost that leaned against the far wall, where the moonlight softly silhouetted them.

Like eight Cakes, thought Emma, *crowded together, sleeping in our little upstairs roost at the bakery.*

Ruby pointed to the three red hens on the highest rung of the roost, their heads stuck under their wings, fast asleep.

"That's Ivy on the left," said Ruby. "She's Rosebud's mama. Next to her is Bess—all she does is eat and complain. And there's Bemmie—she's the mama of those four hens on the next rung down. See 'em? Rosebud's nudged up there with them."

"The orange ones?"

Ruby nodded. "Their names are Parallax, Paratrooper, Parchment, and Parliament."

Emma's eyes widened. "Really?"

"Really!" said Ruby.

"Whyever for?" asked Emma.

"Those were words I was reading in the dictionary when they were born," said Ruby. "I read them the dictionary. They love it. It calms them. I've been through the dictionary three times now."

Dove was the friend who first saw Ruby reading the dictionary to her chickens. Dove understood Ruby's delicious acquired taste.

"You think *I* talk a lot!" said Ruby, as if Emma had said so. "Wait until you meet Dove! She'll be back to visit next summer."

"You do talk a lot," said Emma, who had not been thinking that at all, "but I don't mind."

Ruby realized with a jolt that she had been starved for this friend. To think that she had almost lost her! Lucky she had course-corrected in time. She was proud of herself for that. She *was* good at this friend business.

"Herman is the Four Ps' daddy," she was saying now. "He's Rosebud's daddy as well."

"Where is Herman?" Emma asked.

"Banished!" Ruby declared. "Actually, he's a rooster so he lives over at the Butterfields' house, along with Elvis. Elvis is Bemmie's boy."

Emma shook her head. "I'm so confused."

"It's confusing until you live with them. They're a family, even if they don't all live together. And Miss Eula and me, we're their family. Miss Eula is their grandmother, too. I used to have a grandfather but he died two years ago. It was the saddest thing ever. Accident. Bridge. Grief. I still can't talk about it."

Emma thought she was talking about it just fine. "I'm so sorry," she said.

"Do you have a grandfather?" Ruby asked.

"Yes," was all Emma said. She did not say *Archibald Carrot Cake, Blue Ribbon Bona Fide Grand Champion Baker and Citizen of the World.* She did not know him or her other grandfather. They had died before she was born. She was sorry about that, too.

"I have five brothers and a mom and dad," she finally said.

"You have way too many brothers," Ruby told her.

"You said Ben is cute," Emma reminded her friend.

"I was crazy," said Ruby. "I've course-corrected. But did you see Frances? She's already in love with Ben. She moons over him! I don't know how he can stand it!"

"Who's Frances?" It was easy to forget; there were so many kids in this new place.

"She calls herself Finesse now, but she's just Frances Schotz, great-granddaughter of Parting Schotz, who owns the barbershop in town. Frances comes here for the summer but she lives in Jackson—that's about an hour away—and she goes to the Lanyard School there and takes too much French and too much drama. Melba Jane wants to be just like her."

Emma remembered—Finesse, the girl like Annie, but not. "She invited me to a party tomorrow! The Dr. Dan Deavers Going-Away Soiree!"

Ruby rolled her eyes. "Are you going?"

"I said I would . . ."

"Well, prepare yourself. It will be the most . . . the most . . ." Ruby thought a moment and then came up with the word that had eluded her. "The most *mundane* thing you've ever done. I read that word to the chickens yesterday. 'Lacking interest or excitement.' *Mundane*. In fact," Ruby added, "it will be worse than mundane."

"What's worse than mundane?"

"Comatose. That's when you're not even conscious! And you won't be when Finesse starts her interpretive dance. It goes on for hours. And the last time she did one, she ran into House and broke his arm! It's no wonder he ruined it again in the All-Stars game. It wasn't completely healed up yet."

The Four P's and Rosebud began to murmur and stir on the second rung of the roost.

"Cousins," said Ruby, nodding. "Let's let them sleep."

"Good night, girls," whispered Emma. She wasn't sure

what to make of these pet chickens, not to mention this
kooky friend, but she was not at all surprised, in this new
world, to find that her heart was beating that calm way it
beat when all was well with the world.

Gone was her hesitation. Gone was any hint of a question about making a new friend. She'd made one, *the* one,
not an acquaintance, but a best friend. Someone to share
secrets with and have adventures with and figure out the
world with. Here she was, and in this astonishing, mysterious new place.

She knew she was risking her heart, but she also knew
she was just going to do it. *Yes. Please. Again.*

∽ Chapter Sixteen ∽

So there they stood, Ruby and Emma, outside the green-house, under the moon, between yes and no, over the hard part, in the beginning of a brand-new friendship.

A dog howled from the direction of town.

"Hale-Bopp," guessed Ruby. "Howling at the moon!"

"Sounds like it," said Emma.

Lights winked on inside the Pink Palace.

"I should go home," Emma finally said.

"Me too," said Ruby. "I live next door with my mama."

But instead of going home, Ruby walked to the back porch of the Pink Palace and sat on the steps. Without a word, Emma joined her. They weren't ready to leave each other. They didn't even need language to say so. That was the mark of a true friend.

A billowy breeze played across Emma's shoulders. She let her thoughts wander. "I'll bet you've lived here all your life," she said. "I'll bet you were born here."

"That's the truth of it," said Ruby. She scratched at a mosquito bite on her big toe.

"I'll bet you've only lived in one house your whole life, the one next door."

"Yep," said Ruby, "although I live plenty in the Pink Palace, too."

"I think it's magical, to belong to one place," said Emma. "A place. Some place. Any place."

Ruby hooted. "There's not one thing magical about Halleluia, Mississippi! It's mundane, Emma. Not comatose, but definitely mundane."

"I don't think it's mundane at *all*," said Emma. "You've got chickens and a Pink Palace and you work in a store, and you play baseball, and you know all the kids and all the stories of this town and you have friends you miss who come visit you, too!"

Ruby shook her head. "But I never go anywhere, or do anything. It's the same old thing, day after day."

Emma sighed. "That sounds perfect."

Ruby laughed. "You must be from a town even smaller and more mundane than Halleluia, and that's saying something. You must think this is the big city!"

"It's not that," said Emma. She made her voice very quiet. "The truth is, I've moved so many times, I don't know where I'm from."

Ruby sat up straight. "Don't you have people? Grandparents, aunts, uncles, cousins?"

Emma stared at her feet, not sure how much to tell. Should she recite the names of the many great-greats whose names were on the itemized grocery lists and lined index cards her family carried from place to place, and who were the originators, many years ago, of the Cake family's most treasured recipes?

Mavis Oatmeal Raisin Muffin Cake. Willa It's-So-Dusty-I'm-Exhausted Cake. William Macaroons-Out-Your-Ears Cake. And that was just the beginning. She couldn't explain why they had no choice but to keep moving, because she couldn't understand it herself.

"We are itinerant bakers," she said softly. It was a risk, to say it. Kids laughed. She and her brothers had learned not to tell.

"What is that?"

Emma sighed. "I can't explain it. We move and we bake. We come to a town when it needs us, and we leave when it doesn't need us anymore. Bakers have moved from town to town for ages, baking and selling their goods. It's just what we do, what we've always done. Our specialty is cake. And mine is soup—for some reason I love soup more than cake. We never stay anywhere long, and we never live anywhere twice."

"Like the Vikings!" said Ruby.

"No," said Emma. "We don't plunder."

"Marco Polo!"

"We're not explorers."

"Like the Thousand and One Arabian Nights!"

"Not exactly," said Emma, "although I have an ancestor named Scheherazade Moroccan-Date Cake who baked for the Arab sheiks."

"Really!" said Ruby. She sat up very straight and tried again.

"Like Wayfaring Strangers!"

"Actually, not far off," said Emma. She had an ancestor, Ethelinda Chocolate Bow-top Caravan Cake, who had lived in Greece. Or was it old Macedonia?

"Cowboys!" said Ruby. "They went everywhere, on cattle drives, like the Old Chisholm Trail. I *love* cowboys."

Emma brightened. "Actually, we have a family story about Lucky Pete Chewy Cowboy Raisin Cake. Cowboys couldn't take chickens on their cattle drives, so they soaked raisins and used raisin water instead of eggs to leaven their cakes. Lucky Pete invented that!"

"You've got amazing ancestors!" Ruby was delighted to have a delicious scrap of family history from her friend. "Your life is more exciting than mine will ever be. The next time you move, take me with you!"

Emma shook her head. "I'm a prisoner of my family's destiny," she said, falling into the melodrama of her life. "You're so *lucky*, Ruby. You can finish a school year and you have friends and a real house of your own—two houses! I've never had one house of my own, not one room of my own! No furniture of my own. No house to paint, no room to stuff with treasures, and my friends can't come visit me—I'm too far away and I move too much. You can't appreciate what it's like to move and move and move without knowing where you belong! I can't even keep a chicken!"

"Good thing," said Ruby.

Emma had to laugh, even though tears stung the back of her nose.

"Well . . ." Ruby said, trying to think of something helpful. "You have four dogs!"

"They're portable," sniffed Emma. "*We're* portable, all of us." She stood up to go.

"Why don't you just stay here, in Halleluia?" asked Ruby. "It's mundane, but you've got a great café now, and a great kitchen, and a great job, and a—"

"It's always great!" Emma interrupted. She raised her hands as if she was trying to stop Ruby from extolling all the virtues of her new temporary home and fixing everything for her. "And then we leave." She gave Ruby a lopsided smile. "So it's not even a good idea to be friends. I'll just have to leave when my dad decides it's time to go."

But Ruby wouldn't hear of not being friends, especially after all she'd had to go through to get this one.

"We'll have to change that," she said. "What can we do to make sure your parents never want to leave Halleluia?"

"Nothing," said Emma. "I've tried everything I know. I've asked, I've begged, I've cried, I've written letters to my dad, nothing works."

"We need a plan," Ruby said. "That's all. We need a plan that will make your parents want to stay. Meet me here in the morning, as soon as you wake up."

Emma shook her head. "I work in the morning, first thing. I'm making soup."

"What kind?"

Emma hesitated. "My specialty," she said, as quietly as possible.

"Chicken," said Ruby with only a hint of accusation in her voice.

"Sorry," said Emma. She walked to the gate and let herself out. *Still friends,* she thought. *I think so.* "See ya," she said, as she clicked shut the gate.

"See ya," said Ruby. And she meant it.

~ Chapter Seventeen ~

Ruby knew she was a welcome back-door visitor and not a customer who needed to use the front door. She appeared in the Cake kitchen early the next morning as if she had been expected. The smell of onions, celery, carrots, spices, and herbs sautéing in olive oil in a giant pan on the giant stove greeted her.

"Just smell all those vegetables!" she crowed to no one in particular.

Arlouin Cake didn't seem surprised to see her. "Good morning, dear," she said with a smile. "Come be of some use, will you?" She led Ruby to the colossal mixing machine. "Just stand here with the mixer and make sure the batter doesn't careen out the bowl. I'll mix in the nuts and raisins and grated carrots next. First, this batter needs to mix for two minutes."

Arlouin went back to the stove and kept sautéing the vegetables Ruby had smelled. "These will make a good soup starter," she called to Ruby as the mixer filled the room with its noise. Ruby watched the batter swirl and dip and cascade up and down in the big metal bowl.

"What do I do if it tries to escape?" she shouted.

"Use the rubber spatula to make it behave!" called Arlouin over her shoulder. "You can do it!"

Ruby found the rubber spatula on the counter and poked at the batter as it tried to climb up the sides of the bowl. "Back!" she yelled at it. "Down, boy!"

Emma came into the room with a huge tub of raisins in front of her. "Found 'em! They were in the upstairs kitchen on top of the fridge." Then she saw Ruby and laughed. "See? You come over here and we'll put you to work!"

"Cream cheese!" called Leo Cake. He came through the back door with enough cream cheese and confectioners' sugar to ice four huge carrot cakes.

Emma took over the sautéing for her soup and Arlouin took over the batter patrol from Ruby. "Thank you, sour-heart!"

Emma's father pulled cake pans from the cake pan drawer and yelled "All Cakes on Deck!" Like magic, the Cake boys appeared.

Jodi and Van cut round circles from paper grocery bags and put them in the bottoms of the cake pans—they needed eight giant paper circles inserted into eight giant cake pans to make four giant layer cakes. Roger opened the raisins and measured them into four equal piles. Ben grated carrots and supervised his brothers.

More carrots, more paper-bag circles, more raisins, and all while Arlouin stirred and Leo poured and Ruby—who saw an opportunity—opened the wide oven doors so the eight round cake pans filled with batter could slide into the ovens and become carrot cake. There wasn't one whine, one shove, one argument. The Cakes worked together like they were in an elaborate ballet—or maybe it was more like a circus act—never in one another's way, hardly speaking, knowing just how much to measure and when to add, stir, pour, and pop into the oven.

It was not the least bit mundane. It was thrilling.

"Well done!" said Leo Cake.

"Soup's on!" Emma announced. She sounded happy, and she was. Her sauté had gone into the soup pot, along with the stock and the chicken she had taken care to make sure Ruby didn't have to see. Now to simmer the soup for a few hours. She'd add the cooked noodles last.

The boys moved to the sink to crash the dishes in order to be released into the day. Their parents would take it from here, and the boys knew when to be back to help with the lunch shift.

"Move over!" whined Roger as the empty metal mixing bowl slipped out of his hands and clanged on the counter.

"Butterfingers!" snarled Jody.

"Stop torturing the whiner," said Van.

"Am not!" whined Roger.

"Are so!" challenged Jody.

Then the pushing started. The cake-making, working-together spell was broken.

Emma took off her apron and caught Ruby's eye. Ruby patted her overalls pocket and mouthed the word *plans*. Emma invited Ruby up to her bedroom.

"Good! Good!" said her father, unable to hide his happiness that his daughter had found a friend. "Excellent!"

Emma gave him a half smile. "I'll be back to stir the soup."

"No need!" said Leo Cake. "I'll stir!"

"You're making cream cheese frosting," Arlouin reminded him.

"I can stir and mix at the same time," he informed her. He shoved his glasses up on the bridge of his nose and waved Emma out of the kitchen.

So much can happen before nine in the morning. The rolls were in their baskets, the soup simmered, and the cakes baked. Bread was rising on breadboards near the ovens and breakfast muffins filled the muffin basket. Arlouin had made her signature pimento cheese, so there would be pimento cheese sandwiches at the Cake Café for lunch, along with soup and rolls and carrot cake until they ran out of everything.

And that's not counting the lemon meringue, coconut, and chocolate cream pies that Leo and Arlouin had taken across the street to the Pine View Café earlier in the morning. Leo and Arlouin were pooped. And the Cake Café would start serving lunch in three hours.

So Arlouin and Leo made themselves pimento cheese sandwiches with day-old bread and poured glasses of lemonade and sat in the lawn chairs out back, under the shade of the silver maple, while the boys played ball and Emma and Ruby schemed upstairs in Emma's bedroom.

Hale-Bopp left the pack of dogs and boys and trotted past Leo and Arlouin and to the back door of the Cake Café. Leo got up to let him inside. It was hot, even for nine in the morning, and Hale-Bopp did not like heat.

"Emma has made a friend," said Leo Cake when he returned. Then he took another bite of his sandwich. "Good batch of pimento cheese!"

"Thank you," answered Arlouin. "And yes, she has."

"I always hate to tear her away," he began.

"She gets so attached," agreed Arlouin.

Leo sighed and took another bite of pimento cheese.

"Didn't you ever get attached when you were a kid, Leo?"

Leo chewed and thought. "Yes. No. I don't remember." But there was a sizzle in his memory that pricked at him.

The boys were hooting and waving now at the arrival of more of their friends.

"Have you ever seen so many kids in one place right outside our back door?" asked Arlouin.

"I don't believe I have," said Leo. "But then, we've had lots of back doors in our time."

"That we have," agreed Arlouin. She watched Gordon and Honey take off Eudora Welty's tutu so Gordon could put it on. The dog seemed relieved to relinquish it.

"The people here are so friendly, too," said Arlouin.

Leo nodded.

"The first itinerant Cake," said Arlouin. "Tell me again—what was his name?"

"Theopholus Bardito Cake," Leo answered with pride. "He blew in with a warm wind—and a wispy Cake fog—generations ago somewhere in the ancient Ottoman Empire. Constantinople, I think. I don't remember. He baked bread for the sultan! He was married to Marvella the Magnificent, who made the first cakes.

"I wonder if they had children," Arlouin said, as an afterthought, as she watched Jody hit a line drive to second.

"Well, of course they did," said Leo, "or I wouldn't be here."

"How long do you think we'll stay?" asked Arlouin, finally.

"Well," said her husband. He drained his lemonade. "Weather patterns are stable and we're just getting started. It's clear we've got good work to do with the Pine View, but I'm not sure this town needs two cafés."

"So I've heard from several visitors this week," said Arlouin.

"I might have mixed up our destination," Leo confessed.

"How so?" asked Arlouin. She sat up straight in her lawn chair.

"Well," said Leo, thoughtfully, still trying to figure it out himself. "I thought I was answering one letter, but somehow I must have mixed up the addresses—we're here, and this place feels so familiar to me. But we never go anywhere twice. If I didn't know better, I'd say I was here before."

"That's because we move so often it's hard to remember," said Arlouin. "I can tell you we've never been in this town before. But we do move more and more frequently now, Leo, and honestly, family lore notwithstanding, it sometimes feels as if you're running from something."

"I don't run *from* anything. I run *to*."

Leo took off his glasses and cleaned them with his napkin. When he put them back on, he shoved them up on his nose with his index finger and said:

"Day by day and night by night we were together. All else has long been forgotten by me."

"Oh my," said Arlouin. "What is that?"

"I don't know," said Leo. "It came into my head as we set off on this move, like it's something I'm supposed to remember."

~ Chapter Eighteen ~

Upstairs in Emma's bedroom, Hale-Bopp plopped himself on the wood floor in order to take advantage of the breeze from the attic fan in the hallway. It was a hot breeze, but it was something.

Emma offered Ruby her desk chair while she flopped across her bed on her stomach. Ruby examined the items on Emma's desk: pads of drawing paper, thick and thin; a Composition Book notebook with green rubber bands around it; a mayonnaise jar of sharpened colored pencils; a stapler; a heavy, oversize pair of black-handled scissors; various erasers, fat and pink and brown; a pile of good-bye notes from Emma's friends, tied with a ribbon; a small pile of pushpins for the world map and the US map on the wall; and a clutch of four-by-six-inch lined index cards.

There was also a wooden recipe box spilling over with recipes for Emma's best soups. The box had a chicken painted on it. Of course.

But the Friend Atlas was the star of the room. Ruby needed to get closer to it. She stood so close she could touch it, but out of respect she didn't. There was a sketch of each friend that Emma had left. They were pushpinned onto a handmade map along with descriptions of that friend—her favorite food, their favorite thing to do together, favorite phrases and places and songs and so much more.

"Good garden of peas," said Ruby, awe in her voice. "You really believe in detail! This is . . . I've never seen anything like it."

"I keep adding to it when I think of more," Emma said softly. "That's what the index cards are for."

"I'd really like to know this Marcy," said Ruby. She read from Marcy's index card, pinned under her sketch: *Knows seventy-four riddles. Got sixteen stitches when she fell off her bike. Gave me a lizard for Christmas. Sleeps with her head at the foot of the bed. Once ate my liver for me. (I hate liver, so no recipe.)*

"She was great. IS great," said Emma.

Ruby stared intently at the sketches. "You told me you make soup and you help in the bakery. You didn't tell me you're an artist."

"I'm not an artist," said Emma. "Not really."

"Well, you're good with a pencil. And you sure have moved a lot."

"Yeah," said Emma. "And thanks."

Ruby's hair slopped out of its ponytail. She pushed it out of her face. There were all colors and shades of faces and hair in Emma's colored-pencil sketches; all shapes and sizes of noses and eyes and chins.

"But nobody with red hair," Ruby observed. "Not until now."

"That's right," said Emma.

"Are you going to draw me, too?"

"Do you want me to?"

"Maybe later." Ruby pulled herself away from the Friend Atlas. "First things first."

She plucked a folded piece of paper out of her front overalls pocket. Hale-Bopp heard her unfolding it and came to her side.

"Not so fast, buddy-boy," said Ruby.

Hale-Bopp gave Ruby a sad hound-dog look and slumped like a rag doll back on the floor, his angles and bones clattering against the old wood.

"I made you a list," Ruby told her friend. "Here's how not to leave Halleluia. This is a list of things that make it hard to leave any place. I'll read it to you."

Emma scrunched a pillow in her arms. "Ready." Ruby pulled the desk chair over to the bed and sat on it. She cleared her throat.

"Death."

Emma sat up straight. "What?"

"Well, if you die, you don't leave."

"What?"

"It doesn't have to be you. Snowberger's Funeral Home does the best funerals in the county and Comfort Snowberger—she's our age—writes the Life Notice for the paper . . ."

"Out of the question," said Emma flatly.

"I didn't say these were good things," said Ruby, "just things that make it hard to leave. Next: getting married."

"What?"

"Not you! But we could figure out who is getting married around here and we could make sure you are part of the wedding—you know, flower girl or brides-maid or something. Does the café do wedding cakes? Your folks will stay here so you can go to the slew of weddings you're in, and they will be so used to living here—and the cake business will be so good—they won't want to leave."

"It doesn't work that way," said Emma. Obviously, this girl Ruby was nuts.

"How does it work, then?" asked Ruby. Obviously, this girl Emma had never learned to brainstorm.

Emma turned on her dresser fan. The corner of her Friend Atlas flapped and she got up to tape it securely against the wall. The sketches of her friends bounced in the breeze as she considered her response.

"We stay until we're done with the job," she said.

"What job?"

"The baking job, I guess. One day I'll come home from school, or from my best friend's house, and my parents are packing. It's time to go. Job's done."

"Just like that? How can that happen?"

"I don't know! It just does."

Ruby produced a pencil from her overalls pocket,

put her paper on her knee, scratched through "Death" and "Getting Married" and began to scribble something new.

"What?" Emma asked again.

"I know what you need to do," Ruby replied.

"Tell me."

"You need to have a baby."

Emma rolled right off the bed and headed for her bedroom door. Hale-Bopp followed her. "This conversation is over," she said. "I have soup to stir."

"No, no!" Ruby exclaimed. "I'm serious! I have chickens, I'm a chicken mama—do you see what I'm saying?"

Emma stopped at the door.

Ruby went on. "Your dogs are no good, because—like you said—they're portable."

"*And* they belong to the whole family," Emma pointed out. She let Hale-Bopp kiss her fingers. "To the boys, really . . ."

"Well, I know the kind of babies that can't go with you," Ruby said. "And a good mother doesn't abandon her babies."

Emma was frustrated now. "*What?* Spit it out!"

"You need a garden," said Ruby. "A garden that's all yours, that's full of flowers for the tables downstairs and flowers for Snowberger's Funeral Home and flowers for the Pine View and flowers for teachers' desks and church altars and for putting on gravestones in the cemeteries and for big parties and celebrations and flowers for no reason at all. Flowers."

Emma was unsure. "Flowers? A garden? I don't know the first thing about making a garden."

"Me neither," Ruby admitted. "But I know someone who does. My mama is the county extension agent for gardens. She's got a huge garden. We can ask her how to do it. People are always calling her and asking her how to plant the peas and fertilize the zinnias and make stuff with their mounds of zucchini. And she could never take her garden with her if we had to move!" Ruby stood up and waved her note. "Ta-da!"

Hale-Bopp helped himself. He ate Ruby's note in one soft-lipped gulp.

"Hey! Stop!"

"He does that," said Emma, amused. And then, "I don't want to grow flowers. But I would grow vegetables! For my soups!" She felt hopeful, for the first time.

"Vegetables! Even better," said Ruby. "Vegetable babies!" She shooed Hale-Bopp out the door and stood in front of Emma's Friend Atlas. She put a bright-red pin in Mississippi.

"This is the last pin you'll ever need for this atlas." She crossed her arms triumphantly and smiled at Emma, a huge Ruby Lavender smile.

"Now," she said. "Draw me."

And Emma did.

∽ Chapter Nineteen ∽

Ruby disappeared, to do "reconnaissance work," as she called it. "We have a secret now," she whispered. "Don't tell a soul." Then, as she exited the back door of the Cake Café with Hale-Bopp behind her, she hollered, "I'll see you after the party!"

The soup was scrumptious. Everyone said so. And everyone included Miss Mattie and the clutch of customers who came through the front door of the Cake Café for lunch that day.

"Come in! Come in!" Arlouin welcomed each curious customer. The Cake boys walked the sidewalks like town criers with samples and invited folks to stop by, which they did. The atmosphere was festive.

"It's another experimental week," said Leo Cake from behind the glass counter. "Pay what you can or want, and sample everything! Grand Opening next week! Or so!"

Folks tried a bit of everything. Large slices of warm carrot cake with cream cheese frosting were consumed. Everyone chewed and nodded appreciatively. They sipped soup with the crusty rolls that Emma's mother and father had made early that morning, rolls that sat in baskets at the glass counter next to slices of yesterday's lemon pound cake and a few leftover homemade moon pies all waiting for customers to seize upon.

Gordon—who could not tell time—had ridiculously seized upon a crusty roll for each sticky hand as he scooted out the back door of the café to meet Honey on the ball field for dance practice, only Honey would not arrive for another hour.

"It's time for the boys and girls!" he cried as he ran across the sandy lane too early after lunchtime for the gaggle of kids to reappear, but that didn't matter; he was outside. Spiffy, Alice, Bo-Bo, and Hale-Bopp loped and galloped after him, hoping for some crumbs.

Emma had two pieces of cake and a bowl of her famous chicken soup. After the lunch rush, she helped her parents make the enormous half-sheet cake that would yield fifty pieces of cake for the soiree at Pip's later in the afternoon. "Plenty for a pot-luck party," said Leo, "when there will be so much other food." The cake was baking in the oven while her parents napped upstairs.

Emma was already dreaming about vegetable babies in a garden bed, a solid place to cultivate every day—although she had no idea what that really meant. But it was a start. It was forward motion. It was a plan.

When you were a kid, grown-ups could just pick you up and move you whenever they chose to go. But maybe now, now that she was eleven, she could make her own decisions about staying, and could convince her parents to stay as well. A plan that ambitious would require Ben's help.

So even though she wasn't supposed to tell anyone, she told her brother Ben. They were wiping down tables and locking the front doors, turning around the OPEN sign to the side that said, *We close after lunch but DO come back in the morning for breakfast! You never know what you're going to get!*

Jody, Van, and Roger had finished crashing the dishes and were lying with Gordon under the chinaberry tree next to the schoolhouse, on the far side of the ball field, swatting flies and trying to feel a breeze after the lunch hour of helping-helping-helping and after too many slices of carrot cake.

Spiffy, Alice, Bo-Bo, and Hale-Bopp flopped near them. They looked like a passel of puppies and people trying to survive the afternoon heat, panting and swatting and dozing in the shade.

Gordon, who had the youngest and purest heart of all the Cakes, spoke first. "I want to stay here forever," he said. His brothers looked at one another with surprise. For the first time, Gordon's thought turned out to be the same thought they were having.

"I like it here, too," said Jody, sighing like the angels, declaring this place to be heaven.

"We're just going to have to move again," whined Roger in his bleakest black-forest whine.

"When will the boys and girls come back?" Gordon asked.

"Later, when it isn't so hot," Jody informed his littlest brother. Then he sighed. "Maybe we *could* stay." Jody was ten and knew a thing or two about moving. It had never bothered him before, but suddenly he found himself longing to stay right on this spot, in Halleluia, Mississippi.

Roger had moved just enough times in his seven years to know that's how it worked in his family. "*We always move,*" he said, his voice choked with gloom.

Van held on to his eight-year-old confidence. "I don't mind it," he declared. But now, listening to his clutch of like-minded brothers, he wondered if he did.

Meanwhile, back in the café, Ben told Emma, "It's just what we do," as she poured them both lemonades in the kitchen and they sat at the prep table. "I never thought about whether or not I wanted to move, I just did it because that's what we do."

"Well, I don't want to anymore," said Emma. "I like it here."

"You like it everywhere we go," Ben pointed out.

"Ruby Lavender thinks you're cute," countered Emma.

Ben's face turned watermelon red.

"That's the bossiest girl I ever met!" he fumed. "I've got to find a way out of that job at Miss Mattie's. Maybe we *will* move soon!"

"I thought she was a good ballplayer," said Emma.

"She is," admitted her brother. "She's a great ballplayer, actually." His face colored more deeply, but Emma decided it was a blush of admiration.

"And there are all the other kids," said Emma. "Whenever we can't find you, we know you're at House's house."

"I like him," Ben said. "He can't play right now because of his elbow, but he's a good coach. We're gonna trade baseball cards next weekend."

"And Gordon likes Honey," said Emma.

"And Van and Jody and Roger have made a lot of friends," acknowledged Ben, wondering if he missed always being in sync with his brothers, always being Lord Baltimore, in command. He decided he didn't. It was different, branching out on his own, but it was good, too. And there were so many kids! His brothers had hardly noticed his absence.

"Won't you help me?" asked Emma.

"What do you want me to do?"

"Help me make a garden," said Emma. "Something permanent. Something that's mine. Something I have to stay here for."

That didn't sound so hard. And, Ben decided impulsively, he wanted something, too. He didn't dare talk to his brothers about it. They would tease him. They would be merciless. But he had a sister—and she was a girl! Why hadn't he thought of it before? She could help.

"I'll help you," he said, "if you'll help me with something."

Emma beamed. "Anything. What is it?"

"There's a party this afternoon at Mr. Pip's barbershop, for Finesse's uncle."

"I know," said Emma. "I'm going. It's a soiree."

"It's a party," said Ben, ever the realist. "I don't want to go, but Mom says, 'Cakes will make an appearance!' so I need you to help me." He picked up the broom and began to sweep the floor, even though it had already been swept.

"With what?" Emma got up and hung the wet washcloths and dish towels on their pegs by the sink to dry. Her brothers never remembered to do this. She checked the timer for the cake.

Ben stopped sweeping and held tightly on to the broomstick with both hands. "I need you to help me."

"Yes?"

"With."

"With what?"

"*With a girl.*" His gut hurt when he said it. He thought of running out of the room. Instead, he stared at his broomstick as if it was holding him to the spot.

"Ruby?" asked Emma. This was too easy.

"No," said her brother. He took a breath. "Finesse."

"Oh!" Emma had been so fixated on her own problems, she had failed to notice her brother's. But now she remembered what Ruby had said the night before. *She's already in love with Ben. She moons over him! I don't know how he can stand it!*

This town was not the least bit mundane. But it would not do to let Ben know that she knew what everyone else knew.

So instead she sat at the table again and asked, "Why?" in her most innocent voice.

There's no easy way to say it, thought Benjamin Lord Baltimore Cake.

"She wants to be my girlfriend. She loves me," he blurted. Now his face was on fire. He walked the broom back to its perch by the back door and bopped his forehead on the door three times.

Emma choked on the last of her lemonade. But that was Ben. Direct. And, like Ruby Lavender, most likely misinformed.

"How can you tell?" she asked when she could talk again.

Ben walked back to the prep table. He would not elaborate. "You haven't been paying attention," was all he would say about it. "I'll help you with your garden. Can you help me?"

"What do you want me to do?"

"Just steer her away from me at the party, will you?"

"How am I supposed to do that?"

"I don't know! Tell her I'm awful! Tell her terrible things about me."

"But there aren't any terrible things about you, Ben," said Emma. "I mean, you're annoying, but you're my brother. There aren't any really *terrible* things."

"Then make some up!" Ben took their empty glasses to the sink.

"I don't know . . ." Emma wasn't much good at making things up. She was good at being precise, at noticing details and presenting the facts—all you had to do was look at her Friend Atlas to see that.

Ben kept his face turned away from his sister. "It's embarrassing," he said. Couldn't she see that? He wasn't ready for girls. He was ready for baseball.

When Emma didn't reply, he continued. "Everyone at the party will notice! The boys will make fun of me."

Emma scratched at an itchy spot and wrinkled her nose at the thought of running girl-interference for her brother. Since when did girls think her brother was cute? He didn't look cute at all to her, but he did look like he was suffering, and she knew what that felt like.

"Okay," she said. "Consider it done. I'll do it."

She had exactly two hours to figure out how.

~ *Chapter Twenty* ~

Schotz's Barbershop—everyone just called it Pip's—had been a town gathering place for many years. After all, when you're eighty-eight years old and have been cutting the town's hair for over fifty years, you know everybody. And everybody knows you.

Pip's was more than a barbershop, of course. It was big. It was well lighted. It was well informed. It was the most companionable place in Halleluia, Mississippi. People came to Pip's to have their hair cut, colored, straightened, permed, spiked, and what-have-you by Pip or one of his hearty helpers.

Lamar Lackey—who wore his hair in an Afro twist—was best at the old-fashioned shampoos and sets, because he loved everything that had to do with old Hollywood. All the women of a certain age in Halleluia asked for Lamar. He had Phoebe Tolbert in his chair right now.

Hampton Hawes—who wore his hair close-cropped and neat-as-a-pin—could snip and sculpt a beard better than any man alive. And a new hire, Carol Rose Booth, just out of beauty school and working part-time, was the absolute best at the latest lady's cuts.

But Pip! Pip was your everybody's-hair man, your

finger-curl man, your pageboy man, and your *I'm ready for something different* man.

And he was as bald as a cue ball himself.

It pained him that his only great-granddaughter, Frances Schotz ("Please, Poppy, call me Finesse!"), would not let anyone touch her hair this summer. She was a fan of the clip-and-dip, as she called it, and at the moment, her blue tips and clip at the top of her head were her artistic decision. It looked like a blue fountain. "I'm going through my blue period, like Picasso," she'd told her great-grandfather. *"C'est très jolie, n'est-ce pas?"*

No, no, it wasn't pretty, Pip had wanted to tell her, but of course he didn't, because he knew his opinion was that of a traditionalist, for one thing. For another, he knew his great-granddaughter's hair would change soon enough. Last summer it had been cornrowed.

"Poppy!" cried Finesse as she and Melba Jane came through the front door with streamers and helium balloons, all blue. Pip pushed aside the long curtains at the back wall of the store to reveal the party room. Finesse kissed her great-grandfather and sailed into the open back room with her provender, bopping Phoebe Tolbert on the head with the balloons while Mrs. Tolbert sat in Lamar Lackey's chair with foils all over her head.

Mrs. Tolbert was delighted—just one more thing to put in her column tomorrow. *This reporter was attacked— attacked!—by helium balloons when . . .*

Finesse changed the radio station to the oldies station she loved and turned up the volume. "Fly Me to the Moon" morphed into "Land of a Thousand Dances." "Naa, na-na-na-na!" Finesse sang.

Melba Jane was right behind Finesse with a bag of ice and her clipboard. She put down the ice and made a note of the song change as "Land of a Thousand Dances" turned into "Do Wah Diddy Diddy."

Melba gave her hair a pat and sang. "She looked good! She looked fine!"

"Oh, for heaven's sake!" cried Phoebe Tolbert. She usually had her hair done by Melba's mother, at Locks by Leila, outside of town. But she couldn't resist the chance to watch the soiree unfold.

"And the cake is coming from the Cake Café!" Finesse warbled as she sailed into the party room. "It's a *bon voyage gateau*! And Mrs. Wilson is bringing tablecloths from the Sunshine Laundry!"

"I need my notebook!" cried Phoebe Tolbert, waving a desperate hand in the mirror at Lamar Lackey. "It's time to take notes already!" Lamar handed Mrs. Tolbert her big brown purse and kept foiling away, dabbing on Mrs. Tolbert's signature hair color, strawberry blonde.

At the appointed time, the barbers put away their combs and scissors, turned off the dryers, washed out the brushes, and swept up the hair on the floor just before the town arrived with plates of deviled eggs and meat loaf

sandwiches and platters of fried chicken and a mountain of salads: potato salad, green salad, broccoli salad,
macaroni salad, and seven kinds of Jell-O salads shaped
like fluted flying saucers with bits of carrot or nuts or
pineapple suspended in their jiggling orange or green
or yellow orbs.

Tot Ishee brought her homemade pretzels, which no
one would touch but her husband, Ferrell Ishee, Halleluia
School's fourth-grade teacher. Mr. Ishee was known by
most of the town as Tater. Tater and Tot's little girl, just
two years old, was named Martha but was affectionately
called Spud. She careened around the room in a little yellow car that she pushed with her feet. She ran over the toes
of anyone who got too close to her. *She does it on purpose,*
decided Phoebe Tolbert, who positioned herself—for safety
as well as reporting—back in Lamar Lackey's twirling barber chair with her notebook, pen, and perfect hair.

Emma had helped make the Light as a Feather Bon
Voyage Yellow-Yellow Sheet Cake with Sugar-Sugar White
Frosting for the soiree. It had to be frosted and decorated
after the lunch rush, so the Cakes were late bringing over
their masterpiece, which didn't matter because the cake
would be the last thing eaten.

"Remember, you're going to help me," said Ben to Emma
as he hoisted the cake in the Cake kitchen with his father.

"I remember," said Emma. She had no idea what to
expect. She wished she had facts, or a chart, or some

choices—research on how to run interference. She wished she had better instincts about these things.

She had taken the time to write some possibilities on the index cards in her bedroom. She shoved them into her shorts pocket but had little hope of their being helpful.

Ben is such a quiet boy, was one thing she wrote, which was true unless he was fighting with his brothers. She wrote that, too. *Ben leaves his clothes on the floor. Ben eats with his mouth open. Ben likes baseball more than people.* There. That was better. And all true.

"Let's go!" said their father, who had a smear of frosting across one of his glasses lenses. He didn't seem to notice.

Into the barbershop they trooped, every single Cake but Arlouin, who would follow with Gordon. Ben helped his father carry the cake to the back room, to the long, tall, metal table that had been set with Mary Wilson's freshly starched tablecloth and Evelyn Lavender's cut-first-thing-this-morning flowers.

"Wow," said Leo Cake. "This is quite the table!"

"It's from Snowberger's Funeral Home," said Miss Eula as she plopped down her daughter's famous zucchini bread. "They use it for . . . for their work," she said with a solid flourish. She smiled at Ben and Ben nodded back. "The Snowbergers can't come today. They've got a funeral to tend, but you'll meet them soon enough."

Jody, Van, and Roger were right behind Leo and Ben, cleaned up and cranky, carrying fancy plates, froufrou napkins, and a cake cutter and candles, respectively, arguing over who was carrying the most important items.

"Big table!" they chorused.

"It's for dead people," Ben informed them.

The brothers looked around as one, to see if any dead people were being displaced.

"Good afternoon, Benjamin," murmured a radiant Finesse.

Ben shot his sister a knowing look. Emma fished in her pocket for her note cards.

"Ben does not know the names of the states in alphabetical order, but I do!" she told Finesse.

Finesse completely ignored Emma. "I'll bet you helped decorate this beautiful cake!" she said to Ben.

"Oh, he doesn't decorate," said Emma, putting herself between Ben and the cake. "He just does the dishes. Badly. Could you show me where the bathroom is, Finesse?"

"If I have to," answered Finesse, but she kept her eyes on Ben as she gestured to a closed door.

"Frances!" called Pip. "Come fix this radio station!" and that broke the spell.

Arlouin came through the front door carrying Gordon, who was crying because he'd had to take off Eudora Welty's tutu and leave it soaking in the Cakes' kitchen sink. It was filthy, clabbered with mud from the week's play. He summoned a batch of fresh tears when he saw

Honey arrive in her tutu. It had been washed and blocked by Mary Wilson at the Sunshine Laundry.

"I forgot to wash it," said Arlouin to the disconsolate Gordon. "I'm sorry."

"Come here, Sticky Buns," said Emma. "I have a surprise for you."

Mary Wilson waved another tutu as she came in the front door of the barbershop. "I got it!" she said. Cleebo's mother had stitched it up haphazardly from a yard of nylon netting she'd bought from Miss Mattie. "Hope he don't mind white," she said.

Gordon didn't mind at all. He donned the tutu on the spot, and twirled right into the guest of honor, Dr. Dan Deavers himself, who was being cheered into the barbershop by the Aurora County All-Stars.

Finesse forgot about changing the radio station. She was beside herself with glee. "He's out of his coma!" she trilled, "and he's going back on television!" Her hands were clasped under her chin, her eyes shone like the sun, and her smile was as wide as the Mississippi River. This was her moment. She had planned everything to the tiniest detail. The soiree would be stupendous.

Dr. Dan had spent time in Pip's barber chair earlier that day.

"Aren't you getting tired of this style?" Pip had asked, like he always did.

"Don't try to switch me off it," Dr. Dan had said. He always said that. "This is *my* style."

"Well, you're out of style, James Robert," Pip had replied as always, using his grandson's given name.

"I wouldn't be surprised," Dr. Dan had said. As always. "But this is my style and nobody does it like you do. Thank you, Poppy."

Now Dr. Dan came through the door of Schotz's Barbershop with the shiniest hair in Aurora County, all conked and pomaded to beat the band. He looked slick, and he was. He scooped up Gordon and deftly plopped him right into a surprised Phoebe Tolbert's lap, tutu and all. Then he turned to the applauding crowd, his fans.

The Mamas smiled all over their faces. The Papas puffed up, proud. Pip stood beside his grandson the famous actor. Finesse stood by Ben Cake, tipping toward him like the Leaning Tower of Pisa. Emma wormed her way between them and asked Finesse to help her cut the cake. Finesse directed Emma to Melba Jane and her clipboard.

"To the assembled!" Dr. Dan began in his basso profundo voice.

And that's when the dogs got in.

∽ Chapter Twenty-One ∽

It is a truth universally acknowledged that a room filled with good food and bad pretzels must be in want of some chaos.

Especially if Spiffy, Alice, Bo-Bo, and Hale-Bopp missed their breakfast and lunch because of the All-Cakes-on-Deck pie baking, carrot cake making, lunch rushing, and party cake baking (with a hefty dose of friend making thrown in for good measure). Especially if each Cake thought another Cake had fed the dogs. Especially if the doors to the party venue are left wide open, front and back.

If you fill a room with food, hungry dogs will come.

And they did.

All except Eudora Welty, who wasn't hungry, anyway. She'd eaten plenty of Honey's scrambled eggs that morning. She came to the party with her people, was sleeping by the front door of the barbershop, and couldn't be bothered to move from her shady spot.

"It is with a full and yet heavy heart that I leave you!" boomed Dr. Dan, just as Bo-Bo began to love up on him. "And you, too!" said Dr. Dan with a laugh, not yet realizing what was happening.

Right behind Bo-Bo was Alice, then Hale-Bopp, with Spiffy scrabbling up the rear, all of them happily barking and bouncing and weaving around the stunned onlookers and speeding, lickety-split, to the party room at the back of the barbershop, where the smells were the strongest and the meat loaf sandwiches were the first to be swallowed.

"No-no-no!" cried Finesse. Melba dropped her clipboard. The chase was on.

Gordon and Phoebe Tolbert clung to each other as the tide of humanity spun their barber chair in a full circle and followed the dogs to the back room, with everyone shouting and pushing or pulling or ducking aside to make room for the dogs or the Cakes chasing the dogs.

"Bless your hearts, bless your hearts!" Tot Ishee cried, over and again, as she stood near the cake table with her terrible pretzels, her arms raised high with the platter so everyone—human and dog—could froth around her. Pretzels spilled from the platter and onto the floor.

"*Mes amis!*" shouted Finesse, but it was no good. The mayhem was beyond her.

Spud Ishee squealed with delight and rode her yellow car into the middle of the calamity. Mr. Ishee grabbed her. The yellow car spun like a tiny tornado into Mrs. Varnado, who screamed and backed herself into a case of hair clippers.

The radio played "Whole Lotta Shakin' Goin' On" while the dogs chomped and skidded and changed direction, evading capture. The partygoers slipped and skidded and lunged and fell trying to grab a dog or catch a platter that clattered to the floor—there went the fried chicken. The floor was crisscrossed in a dozen different ways as people shouted and dogs barked and there seemed no end to the chaos. The Cake boys shouted the loudest and grabbed the hardest, but their dogs would not be caught. They ran from the party room back out to the barbershop, back into the party room, like out-of-control yo-yos flying through the air.

"My soiree!" cried Finesse. "Somebody help!" She looked around for her great-grandfather but couldn't see him in the bedlam.

"Whoa, doggies!" said Dr. Dan. Spiffy ran past him with a trail of pretzels behind him. He was spitting them out, so he was considerably slowed down. Dr. Dan reached under Spiffy and picked him up just like he'd swooped up Gordon. Phoebe Tolbert gave a yelp as she wondered if Dr. Dan was going to deposit a dog in her lap as well as a small boy. There simply was no room!

But Dr. Dan strode past Phoebe Tolbert, into the party room, and to the back of the barbershop where, with a heroic flourish, he deposited Spiffy outside the back door, just as he saw Ruby Lavender approaching. He gave her one of his megawatt smiles. "Here you go!"

Spiffy plopped onto the ground, his energy spent, and Ruby peered in the back door, into the noise and movement and shouting.

"Good garden of peas!" she whispered. She stuck her notes from her garden reconnaissance mission into her front overalls pocket and took out the zucchini cookie her mother had given her. She fed half of it to a grateful Spiffy, who ate it lying down. It took the taste of pretzel out of his mouth. He'd had a sandwich already, and he was almost full.

Emma managed to snatch Alice by the collar and drag her to the back door. "Help!" she called to Ruby. Ruby tempted Alice with the other half of the zucchini cookie. "Come on, girl!" It worked.

Bo-Bo had not stopped in his pursuit of the party table, even when his collar got caught on the corner of one of Mary Wilson's tablecloths. He pulled the tablecloth right off the punch table along with the plastic punch bowl, the lime sherbet punch, and a clutch of plastic punch glasses. The shouting crescendoed as the punch bowl met the floor.

The crash made the floor slippery and sticky and petrified the dogs. They were easier to catch then. Bo-Bo and Hale-Bopp were still inside. Hale-Bopp had a fried chicken leg in his mouth. Ben, Jody, Van, and Roger moved as one and were assisted by Cleebo, Wilkie Collins, and the Tolbert Twins, and soon all dogs were out the back door, wet and sticky and still hungry.

"Let's get them home and hose them off," said Ben.

The Cake boys immediately began to move in concert.

"Wait!" said a voice from the back door. Finesse. She did not look happy. Ben stopped moving. His lunkhead brothers were impervious to commands from outsiders, however, and moved across Main Street and toward the Cake Café with the dogs. Thank goodness.

Cleebo, Wilkie, and the Tolbert Twins—on instinct, as soon as they saw Finesse—ran around to the front of the barbershop.

Emma had no time to consult the list in her pocket. She would deal with the situation on instinct.

"He's an idiot!" she said of her big brother.

Ruby looked at Emma, confused. Ben raised an eyebrow at his sister.

But Finesse now *knew* Ben was an idiot. "How *could* you!" she spit.

"He's a moron!" said Emma.

"You're not helping," said Ben.

The bile rose in Finesse's throat. Her love for Ben had evaporated.

"You and your family!" she shouted. "You've ruined *everything*!"

"It's not his fault!" said Ruby, even though she hadn't seen what happened. This sudden defense of a boy made her blush.

"You keep out of this!" said Finesse.

"Make me!" said Ruby, now defending herself. She thrust her chin at Finesse and clenched her teeth.

"Yeah!" said Emma, engaged and energized and out of her mind with a wild desire to protect her friend and her brother. Suddenly Finesse looked nothing like Annie. Emma stepped between Ruby-and-Ben and Finesse. She had never done anything remotely like this in her life. It gave her electric shivers. *Now what?* she asked herself.

"Wait a minute!" shouted Ben. "Wait a minute!" He had no idea what to do. But at that very moment, Miss Mattie came striding toward the back door of the barbershop with a mop in her hand from Pip's broom closet. That made up Ben's mind.

"Let's go," commanded Benjamin Lord Baltimore Cake.

The three of them—Emma, Ben, and Ruby—made a run for it.

~ Chapter Twenty-Two ~

Inside the barbershop, folks got busy and righted chairs and picked up spilled flowers and tossed out half-eaten sandwiches. They recovered the surviving plastic cups from the punch bowl disaster and mopped the lime sherbet punch off the floor. They patted on Finesse and told her that the party would go on. Of course it would. It was a wonderful party already.

"Formidable!" said Old Johnny Mercer, one of Finesse's biggest fans, although it sounded like he said *formy-table!*

"What's a soiree without a little mayhem?" asked Sheriff Taylor. "Do you want me to lock up those dogs?" he joked.

Finesse tried a smile but felt tragic instead. *"Tragique,"* she said with a breathy sigh.

Parting Schotz was as meticulous about his floors as Miss Mattie was about hers, and no one was a better mopper than Miss Mattie, so she had grabbed the mop as soon as she'd arrived and seen the chaos, while Miss Eula filled a bucket with soapy water from the barbershop sink.

Finesse accepted all the good wishes and compliments with her usual practiced air of professionalism. She was not a screamer, so she knew it was not the real Finesse who had yelled at Ben Cake. At first, all she could see was her hard work ruined. But she knew better than to be a quitter. If she'd been a quitter, they'd never have had an All-Stars game and pageant.

Her anger fizzled further as she remembered a time in this very room when she had caused some commotion, a year or so ago. And everything had turned out all right. Everything but House's arm, and that would heal, too.

She finally remembered the radio. She turned the dial to Pip's favorite station—"songs for eighty-eight-year-olds!" (where *was* he?)—and Nat King Cole serenaded Finesse, telling her she was unforgettable in every way. Finesse looked into the barbershop mirrors and smiled at her reflection. "I am," she whispered. "Yes, I am. *Oui, je suis!*"

The tenor of the room was almost back to normal, or as close to normal as this soiree would get. Arlouin Cake, however, was still in shock. She stared at the party cake on the party cake table. "Cakes are always professional. Cakes come from a long, distinguished line of itinerant bakers . . ." She trailed off.

"This is nothing!" Dr. Dan told Arlouin. He patted on her in an effort to make her feel better. "You should have seen the party that put me into a coma!"

"Hush, James Robert," ordered Mary Wilson. She patted on Arlouin as well. Mary's husband, Woodrow "Pete" Wilson, had the punch-soaked tablecloth in his arms. "Tablecloths can be washed," he said in an encouraging tone.

Arlouin came out of her reverie and made more apologies and wondered where her husband had gone. At least the cake had stayed on the party table along with most of the food.

"This is not a catastrophe," Miss Eula said in a comforting voice. "It's just some spilled punch."

Miss Mattie, who hated disarray of any kind, doggedly mopped while Miss Eula dried and Finesse said something to Melba Jane, who had found her clipboard but didn't scribble on it. Melba didn't like sudden chaos. It put her into a state of stillness.

The All-Stars stood with their parents, and everyone waited for the next thing to happen in that way you wait when there has been some kind of upset and you know you want to be tender to everyone.

House held Honey in his one good arm and Honey wrapped her arms around House's neck. They stood next to their father, Leonard Jackson, who washed the punch bowl and cups. Tot dried. "Bless your heart," she said whenever House's father handed her a cup. Tot's little girl, Spud, was spirited off to a nap by her father. Her yellow car rolled under Lamar Lackey's barber chair. Lamar took over the mopping from Miss Mattie and she let him.

Cleebo offered to take the punch-bowl tablecloth to the Sunshine Laundry. His father handed him the tablecloth and the keys to the laundry. The Tolbert Twins migrated to their Aunt Phoebe and helped Gordon out of the barber chair. Gordon made a beeline for his mother, who scooped him up in her arms.

Finesse sidled over to her uncle and looked at him expectantly. He would be the one to pull them together again.

"We shall, of course, continue with our celebration," Dr. Dan affirmed in a softly commanding voice. And, indeed, they did.

People made their way to what was left on the party table. Some folks snacked and gossiped while others made a fresh batch of punch in the clean punch bowl.

"Speech! Speech!" called the Mamas as everyone recovered their wits. "Speech!" called the All-Stars.

Dr. Dan cleared his throat. Melba came back to herself. Finesse surveyed the damage. It would not be perfect, no, but it would be the symphony true. After the dazzle of day and all the clangor, there remains what is true, and what is important, and why they are all gathered to celebrate.

Finesse wrapped an arm around the momentarily tenderized Melba Jane. *"Mon petit chou,"* she said.

Melba laid her head on Finesse's shoulder. "I still don't know what that means," she said, "but it's a comfort."

"Yes," said Finesse. "Yes, it is."

Phoebe Tolbert patted her hair, smiled, and opened her notebook.

~ Chapter Twenty-Three ~

No one thought to look under the tall metal table for Parting "Pip" Schotz and Leo Meyer Lemon Cake. Mary Wilson's billowy starched tablecloth reached the floor on either side of the table and made a comfortable temporary tent for them, a respite from all the chaos. The table was so high, they could both sit under it completely upright.

They had clacked heads from either side of the table as they dived under the tablecloth to grab Hale-Bopp. Or was it Alice? In any case, they'd missed the dog and had instead knocked their noggins so hard they both saw stars. They sat down to get their vision back.

While Dr. Dan spoke, and spoke, and while folks ate the delicious cake and drank up all the punch, and while Arlouin and Gordon cut, served, and stayed with the cake because all the other Cakes were gone, Leo and Pip sat under that same table. The sounds from above and around them were muted by the tablecloth. It was almost like being in an alternate universe, and certainly it was just like being in a hidden place, because they *were* hidden, even though they hadn't planned it that way.

As their vision cleared, each could see the other.

"That was some knock!" said Leo Cake. He was as pale as a seashell and held his hands over his ears for some reason, as if the sound of the head-clack had been extra loud. His glasses were riding sideways on his face, and he didn't seem to notice.

"It was," said Pip. He rubbed his old hands over his wrinkled brown face.

Leo stuck out his hand. "I'm Leo Cake," he said, beginning to recover.

Pip took Leo's hand. "I know who you are."

"Well, I'm sure you've heard of me, here in town," said Leo. Now he noticed his glasses were cockeyed and he righted them.

"Oh, I know you," said Pip. "I know you and I remember you."

Leo startled. "You do?" The squeak in his voice made him sound like a six-year-old. He cleared his throat. "You do?"

"Don't you remember me?" Pip's face was wide and open and calm, like a book.

Leo Cake shoved his glasses up with both hands and stared at Parting Schotz. He shook his head. Yes. No. He didn't remember.

"Well, you were just a young'un," said Pip. "How's your daddy, Archibald?"

"He isn't," said Leo, confused. "He left this earth twelve years ago. You knew him?"

"I knew him."

Leo didn't know what to say or even what to ask. He put his hand over the place where his skull had knocked into Pip's. Maybe he was imagining this conversation. It was a hefty knock on the head, after all, and it hurt.

"Wondered when you'd show up again," was all Pip said, and then he was out from under the table and a commandeering presence in his shop.

ᴄ Chapter Twenty-Four ᴄ

While most of Halleluia was patting itself back together at the barbershop, Ben, Emma, and Ruby were making a stellar getaway.

"This way!" yelled Ruby, and her companions followed her without question. The adrenaline rush was terrific—it was as if they'd just escaped sure death, even though the worst thing that could possibly have happened would have been a bit of mopping.

No, thought Emma. The worst was the embarrassment, and her parents were facing that alone right now. She suddenly felt she should go back.

But she didn't. And neither did Ben or Ruby. The excitement of their escape propelled them, hearts racing, legs pumping, as they crossed Main Street with Ruby and darted down a dirt road that meandered away from town.

"Come on!" Ruby yelled, way ahead of them.

"Hey!" Ben yelled back. He didn't like following this girl's orders. Where were they going?

The stitch in Emma's side was awful and she yelled at Ruby to slow down. She was not a runner; she was a soup maker. A cake baker. An artist, if you believed Ruby Lavender. She wished she had her bike.

Ruby slowed to a walk. "We're safe now," she said. "This house"—she pointed to the right as they walked past, panting—"belongs to the Tolbert Twins. And that one up there"—she waved a hand in the general direction of the next house while catching her breath—"that one belongs to Cleebo. They're all up at Pip's. No one will see us."

"We're at the ball fields," Ben observed, looking left and coming to a stop, "just coming to them from another direction."

"That's right," said Ruby. "And down there"—more waving as she stopped walking altogether—"is the Methodist church, the Baptist church, and the fire department. And all the dead Methodists and Baptists in the cemetery."

They were a good ways from Main Street now. There was plenty of vegetation along the road to hide their view of the back of Miss Mattie's and the Cake Café and the ball fields and more, but they could hear the Cake boys along the sandy lane screaming with delight at washing the dogs—and watering themselves—with the hose at the back of Miss Mattie's store, and the dogs barking at them in their play.

Ruby looked squarely at Ben. "Don't you need to go wash your dogs?"

Ben shook his head. He really didn't want to get doused

with the hose right now, even though it was as hot as fluzions.

"You should help them," said Ruby. "Go on. We don't need you."

I should help them, Ben thought. He always did. He knew he should go back to the barbershop and check on his parents and the cake, but he couldn't face Finesse and her anger, so he stood where he was, silent. The dogs barked, the boys shouted, the heat waved.

Ruby, now clearly irritated, interrupted Ben's thoughts. "I'm on a top secret mission with Emma," she stated flatly, "and no boys allowed."

"You are?" Ben asked. He had a headache. He could leave; it would be fine. He'd just go to House's house. Wait, House was at the barbershop.

"You are?" asked Emma. She moved into the shade of a giant privet hedge on the ball field side of the dirt road and squinted at Ruby in the bright-bright sun.

"I've done my reconnaissance," Ruby announced. She patted her front overalls pocket, where she'd stuck a stubby pencil and her notes. Notes that, miraculously, Hale-Bopp hadn't eaten as they were wrangling the dogs out of Pip's.

"Oh!" said Emma. "That!" It seemed like forever ago that they'd talked about the garden plan. "Well . . ." she said, a little catch in her voice, "I told Ben about it."

"What?" Ruby spit.

"About what?" asked Ben.

"About the garden," said Emma. "About staying here and not moving again."

"How could you!" bellowed Ruby.

"We need Ben," said Emma. "And there was no time to ask you before the party. I was going to tell you at the party, but then . . ."

"I don't have to help," said Ben.

"Yes, you do," said Emma. "We need you!"

"No, we don't," said Ruby. She was so angry she was almost in tears. She slapped at her overalls pocket. *"This is all we need,"* she said to Emma. She jerked a thumb at Ben and said, "We don't need *him.*"

Emma stared at Ruby, at her brother, and back to Ruby.

Ruby pushed her unruly hair out of her face, pulled up her errant overalls strap, and gave Emma a serious *make up your mind* look. "We've got work to do," she said, "even though you are a traitor. But that's just the kind of friend I am, Emma. I don't abandon my friends, even when they betray me."

Emma's eyes filled with tears as she swallowed a mouthful of hot dust. "Coming?" shot Ruby. She turned on her heel and stalked down the dirt road toward the dead Methodists.

~ Chapter Twenty-Five ~

"Wait!" Emma ran after Ruby and grabbed her by the arm. Ruby jerked her arm away and kept walking. Her flip-flops stirred up little dust storms behind each determined step.

"Let her go," said Ben. "Some friend, Emma."

"We do need Ben!" Emma called after Ruby. "We need all the help we can get! A garden is a big thing! And Ben said he would help us."

"You didn't say anything about 'us,'" Ben pointed out.

"Forget it!" shouted Ruby. "You're Benedict Arnold! We had a secret!"

"We still have a secret!" yelled Emma. "I promise! And Ben is trustworthy," she yelled louder. "He won't tell anyone anything you don't want told. *Ruby!*"

Ruby stopped and turned, not because she'd heard anything that had changed her mind, but because she was about to walk too far away to keep her friend, and she knew it. Angry as she was, she knew Emma was right that they were going to need help. And beyond that, she'd done all this reconnaissance!

"Your brother is *bossy*," Ruby called. She took some steps toward Emma and gestured in a wild way. "He's always ordering everybody around."

"He doesn't order *me* around!" said Emma. She took steps toward Ruby.

"Not you. Your brothers," said Ruby. "He's a *gang* leader!"

"We're not a gang," called Ben, irritated and hot and thirsty. In three long strides he was as close to Ruby as he wanted to be. Close enough that he didn't have to shout.

"I'm not your problem," he said. "I'm going. You're bossier than I'll ever be!" He picked up a rock from the dirt road, silently named it Ruby, and threw it as far as he could.

Emma thought fast. "What's in the reconnaissance, Ruby? Where can we build a garden?"

Ruby huffed at Emma. What kind of friend told secrets? What kind of friend insisted she include her meathead brother in their secret plans?

"I'm sure we can find a way for all of us to work together," Emma was saying. "Ben, please don't go."

"Stop trying to make peace," Ruby snapped. "I'm not a peaceful person. You forget, I'm not sweet."

Desperation claimed Emma. "I'm sorry I told Ben. I was trying to help us. I want our plan to work!" She shaded her eyes with both hands cupped at her eyebrows. "I don't want to move. I want to stay here and have you as a friend forever. It's important to me!"

Ruby stared at this girl. She recognized her distress. She understood it. But she didn't know what to say.

A bank of thunderclouds gathering on the horizon blocked out some of the sun's sharpness. Emma put down her cupped hands and continued. She didn't have a choice now. She was committed.

"I think I'm meant to stay here," she said. "To live here, never move again. I can't explain it. There was a thing that happened and I heard it and felt it, and I know it, I believe it, and I'm trying to make it happen, or help it happen, or . . . something."

Her heart beat so hard it hurt. Ruby could feel that hurt from where she was standing.

"So I asked Ben to help us, too, and after we get the garden done, you never have to talk to Ben again if you don't want to. Or me."

Ben wanted to hug his sister. She was brave. And now, he could see, she was right, too. It would be good to stay here, never move, grow up in a place where everybody knew you and you knew everybody. Even if he had to share the town with Ruby Lavender.

He stuck his hands in his pockets and looked at the gathering storm clouds. "It's gonna rain."

Ruby kicked at a rock on the dirt road with her flip-flopped foot. What to do? It was so hot. Cold water from the hose right now would feel so good. And she could spray Ben Cake with it for good measure. Maybe she should spray all of them.

Finally she exhaled in a huge sigh. Which made Emma do the same. Relief!

Then, without pulling her notes out of her pocket, Ruby spoke in a rush and kept her eyes on her dusty toes. "I consulted with my mama, and she says you build a garden where there's sun and heat and water and compost, which is good dirt. All you really need's a shovel. And some chickens!"

Emma felt lightheaded, almost giddy. "Chickens?"

"*Chickens,*" Ruby repeated. "They'll peck up the ground for you in no time flat while they look for worms and bugs and scratch up the grass and . . . well . . . do other things." She looked at Ben. "Unmentionables."

Ben rolled his eyes. Ruby rolled her eyes back at Ben. He was not cute.

"We'll need to run some chicken wire to keep them in the area we want dug up, but I can bring them over every day and let them hang out and do their work, and take them home again before dark. It'll be like going on a field trip for them!"

"Where are we going to put this chicken summer camp?" asked Ben.

"Well, there's sun and heat and compost—and a shovel!— in the alley between Miss Mattie's store and the Cake Café, and that's convenient for us. We can build the garden along the far side of the sandy lane, near the ball field, I figure parallel with the third-base line. I was going to take you there, but we can't go over there to plan it with *the gang* outside washing the dogs, using the hose we need for water. I mapped this all out in my notes."

"You can't build a garden there," said Ben.

"And why not?" Ruby held her head up and flared her nostrils on purpose.

"Because we play ball over there, and *the gang* will trample any garden you make! Not on purpose, but . . . we play ball there!"

"Fine!" spouted Ruby. "I didn't say I had it thought through. I just said I knew what we needed and where to find it!"

Darker clouds from the direction of Bay Springs were behind the thunderheads that slid across the sparkling sun and blocked the harshest rays. They put the ground in shadow and brought a breeze with them. It helped to soothe tempers.

"What about seeds?" asked Emma in her most helpful, peaceful voice.

"We need those, too," said Ruby. "Miss Mattie has them at the store, or we can get some from Mama in her garden. She saves seeds."

"Why are we keeping it a secret?" asked Ben. "And how do we keep it a secret if it's on the third-base line, anyway? Are you just going to have it magically pop up out of nowhere one morning?"

Ruby had a headache now, too. "You're impossible," she

151

said. Obviously, this boy knew nothing about the difference between secretly planning and publicly doing.

"I know a better place," said Ben. Obviously, this girl was a screwball.

"Okay, hotshot," snapped Ruby. "Where is it? You're hired."

Emma exhaled. She didn't realize she'd been holding her breath.

Ben knew exactly what to do. "Follow me."

"See? We do need him," Emma said, coaxing Ruby to come with them.

Ruby made a growling sound. She did not like following a boy's orders, and besides, this boy was impossible.

But Ben Cake was not impossible, no more than Ruby Lavender was a screwball, no more than Emma Lane Cake was Benedict Arnold.

They walked down the dirt road past the churches and took the left fork past Halleluia School and walked to where the road hugged the piney woods.

There, Ben walked right off the road and into the thick green forest. He disappeared among the pines.

THE AURORA COUNTY NEWS

HAPPENINGS IN HALLELUIA

special edition
compiled and reported by
Phoebe "Scoop" Tolbert

Well! *Angel in My Pocket* notwithstanding in this town (I am referring to the end of that movie when everything in the town works out fine), we had a doozy of a disaster at the Dr. Dan Deavers Going-Away Soiree yesterday! This reporter got multiple scoops, in fact so many while sitting in Lamar Lackey's Barber Chair at Schotz's Barbershop (the scene of the crime . . . er . . . soiree), she must write this as a numbered list in order to get this to the paper by deadline.

And I have such short space this week! Note to *Aurora County News* publisher/editor Plas Johnson: MORE SPACE IS NEEDED TO TELL OUR COMPELLING TOWN STORIES! (Readers, please write in with your support.)

But I digress. Herewith and hereto:

1. Frances Schotz is a decorator and soiree planner extraordinaire. It is not her fault that all her stellar planning was sabotaged by wild animals.

2. Dr. Dan's speech was . . . long. Ahem. It included an oration—a declamation, really—about the events leading to his coma on the (so-so) soap opera *Each Life Daily Turns*, and after all that haranguing, he still would not tell us whodunnit.

3. Jerome Fountainbleu arrived late, looking morose. The rumor (substantiated) is, customers say his pies from the Cakes suddenly aren't quite the same as those made by Misanthrope Watkins. Diners are commenting privately. I know.

4. Misanthrope Watkins, formerly pie maker for the Pine View, recently retired, recently seen in the back kitchen at the Cake Café, was also present. She was seen conferring with Arlouin Cake, at length

and with great intensity. This reporter shooed Agnes Fellows over to hear what was being said, but forgot how deaf poor Agnes is.

5. Parting Schotz, known colloquially, locally, as Pip, was missing for an ice age and then suddenly popped out—literally! like a Pop-Tart!—from under the party table (an embalming table on loan from Snowberger's) and proceeded to act as if *that* was not an unusual act.

6. Frances Schotz almost fainted with relief. Her assistant, Melba Jane Latham, fanned her with a handkerchief until Frances was herself again. This, after Frances screamed at the Cake boys (and girl) about the canine mayhem. She did seem to become absolutely serene later.

7. Emerging from under the table just after Pip was Leo Meyer Lemon Cake! This reporter had to leave her barber chair to witness this emerging—both emergings—in their entirety, and to poll the eyewitnesses for local color.

8. The cake was delicious, it must be admitted.

9. The pretzels were not touched, my blueberry congealed salad was the best of the Jell-O salads (would have won a prize), and in the end there were no leftovers. Except pretzels. Which, many noted, were spirited away by Ferrell Ishee when he took his terrorizing tot home for her nap.

10. Conclusion: The Cake Family, new to this town, may be exquisite bakers, but there is more, shall we say, nefariousness to them than meets the eye. Tête-à-têtes with Misanthrope Watkins. Clandestine meetings between Parting Schotz and Leo Cake under the party table. Not to mention feral beasts crashing soirees and the general unhappiness suddenly pervading the Pine View and Jerome Fountainbleu. It must be concluded by any astute observer that the Cakes are becoming liabilities in this town.

(Aside): I have been informed that I would have more space to report if I would cease sending in so many special reports and cease being so long-winded (the nerve!). "Be brief!" said Mr. Johnson. "Brief!"

What about Freedom of the Press? Freedom of Expression! I have so many expressions! And I do need more room. Readers! Write in!

Yours faithfully as I
uncover the mystery, PT

~ Chapter Twenty-Six ~

The girls held back a moment, and then Ruby, calmer now, took a step into the woods and Emma followed. One thing about Ben Cake, thought Ruby: He certainly was not mundane.

"Wait up!" Ruby called to Ben. She trod gingerly in her flip-flops over pinecones and pine straw and fallen twigs and branches and holes where squirrels hid their nuts, until she saw a path ahead, which was where Ben waited for Ruby and Emma.

"Paths are good," Emma said to no one, brushing pine straw from her shirt.

It was instantly cooler in the woods. The breeze that came with the darkening clouds helped Ruby think better.

"I know where we are," she said. "This is the way to the ball fields." She cocked her thumb to the right. "And this—this is the way to House's house."

"Yep," said Ben. "And it's also the way to another house before you get to House's, one that has a garden. It's just . . . well . . . overgrown."

Ruby swallowed. She knew which one. "Norwood Boyd's?"

"I don't know whose it is," said Ben. "It's abandoned."

"That's because it's haunted," Ruby informed him.

"I like the idea of putting the garden near the ball fields," said Emma in a decisive voice. "Especially if there are ghosts in these woods."

However, as she walked farther into the trees, all thoughts of danger or ghosts left her and instead a feeling of welcome began to grow in her heart. She paid attention to it. She recognized it.

Emma, Ruby, and Ben walked on the woods path through dappled light and birdsong. It was as quiet as a church, suddenly, their footfalls muffled by pine needles on the dirt path, their breathing shallow and soft. The smell of pine was clean and strong, and in spite of the earlier hostilities, their spirits lifted. A stiff breeze began to rattle through the trees and Emma looked up to watch the treetops dance.

"There are huge iron gates around the front of the house," said Ben. "Farther down, along the road. This is the quickest way to get there, from the back."

"Kids on the road run past the house without stopping," said Ruby. "'Mean Man Boyd,' they called Mr. Norwood. That blockhead Cleebo called him 'Baby-Eater Boyd.'"

"Really?" said Ben.

Emma shivered. But she didn't want to go back. She was a practical thinker, yes, but this welcoming feeling . . . it was almost spoken. Whose words? Where were they coming from?

"Yep," said Ruby. She enjoyed having someone new to tell the story to. "Norwood Boyd died in that house not long ago."

"Really!" said Ben.

"Really," said Ruby. "House told us so. He told the whole All-Stars team. And Miss Mattie told us the truth of it, too, after the game."

Emma realized there were no markers of any kind to tell them where they were. No house, no road. Just a woods path. She slowed her pace and let Ben and Ruby get ahead of her, to let the wonder of this woods seep into her. Then she hurried and caught up with her companions. It would not do to get lost out here now.

They rounded a curve, came into a clearing, and there it was: a huge, rambling two-story house with gables and a turret making up a third floor, like something out of a fairy tale or a myth, like Sinbad or Rose Red or Hansel and Gretel.

Menacing, thought Ruby. She'd always thought that.

But Emma was of a different mind. She stumbled over a root and Ben helped her up. She couldn't keep her eyes off the house. It was a house built for generations of Cakes, and she knew it. Scheherazade, Ethelinda, Theopholus, Marvella, even Lucky Pete would have wanted to live here and never leave, if only they could have found it.

Emma, Ben, and Ruby walked all the way around the tall iron fence in a wide berth as the path led them to a long, pebbled driveway that ran from the dirt road up to the gates. Now they could see the house from the front.

It was badly in need of paint, with crooked shutters, a collapsing front porch, and massive, ornately carved iron gates at the end of the driveway. The gates had been recently covered in kudzu, from the looks of it—vines were chopped and scattered all around the wide-open gates.

"I don't want to go in there," said Ruby.

"The garden's on the side, over there," Ben said. "I stumbled over the garden fence last week when I was coming home in the dark and got turned around."

"Nope," said Ruby. "This will not do."

But Emma was enchanted.

"This will do just fine," said Emma Lane Cake.

The house wasn't haunted, not at all. It was lonely—Emma could feel it. Whatever had happened here, it had happened lovingly. And now the house was empty. It was waiting for someone. It was waiting for her. It was welcoming her, calling to her. It had been the house all along.

A fat crow called from a high pine tree. Emma walked through Norwood Boyd's imposing gates all by herself, eyes wide and heart bursting. She left Ruby and Ben staring after her.

"It's perfect," Emma whispered. "Perfect."

"What are you doing?" Ruby called to her.

"I'm coming home," Emma said, too soft for Ruby to hear. With each step she took toward the house, tiny grasshoppers leaped out of her way and the stubbly dry grass—such as it was—crunched underfoot.

This is my house, thought Emma. It had been waiting for her for such a long time, and finally Emma had come.

"This is private property!" yelled Ruby.

"Yes," said Emma, still in that small voice. "Mine."

Ruby turned to Ben. *"Do something!"*

Ben shrugged. "I'm gonna visit the garden. In the daylight. I've been hired to create something permanent. Wanna come?"

He followed his sister through the gates.

~ Chapter Twenty-Seven ~

There was a garden; this was true. And it was in a spot where trees had been cleared long ago. It was a big garden, too. It had once been neat and fenced with pretty white pickets, tall and straight. Now the fence had missing pickets and leaning pickets and pickets the color of stained teeth.

The long garden rows, once straight, were now choked with weeds. Chickweed, pokeweed, dockweed, creeping thistle, buttercups, oxeye daisies, clover, and giant dandelions grew every which way along with a few slender volunteer trees. Tall and short and fat and skinny and thorny and smooth, all of them waved hello in the gusting wind.

No one had done any gardening here in years, but it hadn't been *decades*. It was a salvageable garden.

The air was thick with the scent of rain, but no one was paying attention to a thing as mundane as weather. The whorling wind was a welcome relief from the scorching temperatures of the past weeks.

"How did you even know this was a garden once upon a time?" asked Ruby, incredulous.

"House told me," said Ben. "Could your chickens do their thing here?"

"Sure, they could," said Ruby. "And it's already fenced." Now that she was on the other side of the iron gates, and now that nothing spooky had happened to her, she was feeling more sure of Miss Mattie's and House's stories and less sure of the many haunted, monster stories the Aurora County kids had made up about this house over the years. Still, it looked dreary, and more than a little scary.

But not to Emma. While Ruby and Ben contemplated the garden, Emma was captured by the sight of the silver maple trees—there were eight of them, *like eight Cakes*, surrounding the house, majestically tall and lush and full. Just like the tree outside the Cake Café. It could not be a coincidence.

The trees surrounded the house like benevolent caretakers. They shaded the porches and kissed the highest points of the roof in the wind. They invited Emma to climb out of the turret window and onto their graceful branches.

She placed her hand gently on the tree closest to her and felt its warm, rough pulse under her fingertips. What was happening here? *Ka-thump, ka-thump, ka-thump* went her heart. *All's well.*

There was a wide, welcoming yard with bristly old grass and patches of moss front and back. Emma began to look for a way to get up onto the front porch—the stairs were missing—and was surprised by a snuffling and then a sneeze that came from the giant honeysuckle bush by the corner of the porch. She got on her hands and knees and saw that there was a cavernous hole inside the honey-suckle, and in that hole was . . . a dog.

"Eudora Welty!" Emma cried. Instead of pulling the dog out, she instinctively got into the hole in the bush with the old dog. Eudora sneezed once again and then licked Emma's hand with her short pug tongue. Emma scratched Eudora behind the ears and asked, "What are you doing here?"

"YouDoggie!" called a girl's voice. "I know you're here!"

Seconds later, Emma and Honey found themselves eye-to-eye inside the honeysuckle bush cave.

"Hey!" shouted Honey.

"Hey!" shouted Emma.

"Hey!" shouted Gordon right behind Honey.

Eudora sneezed.

"Hey!" shouted House. He waved at Ben and Ruby. "What are y'all doing here?"

"What are *you* doing here?!" asked Ruby. The first grumbles of thunder rolled over the woods.

"All that party commotion scared Eudora," said House, with no blame in his voice, "and she ran away from the party. We knew she'd come here—she always does—so we came to get her on our way home."

A sprinkling of rain began to fall as the wind swooped, the temperature dropped, and the downdraft came in.

"Storm!" yelled Ruby just as the loudest clap of thun-der they'd ever heard—it must have been directly over them—split the sky with its snap, like a whip, and filled the air with the smell of silver.

Emma, Honey, and Gordon leaped from the honeysuckle bush like they'd been shot out of a cannon. Eudora Welty yelped and plastered herself to the back of the bush. Emma ran back inside the bush, scooped the dog under her belly, and struggled back out with her. "C'mon, Gordon! C'mon, Honey!"

She ran smack into House coming to get his dog and they twirled around as if square-dancing with a petrified pooch. House lost his baseball cap. He held out his sore arm in its sling and tried not to let Emma or Eudora hit it. It took some fancy footwork.

"Here!" said Emma. House took his squirming dog under his good arm as the sky opened and rain came down in sheets. Emma snatched up House's cap and scooped up Gordon, who was shrieking. She grabbed Honey by the hand and raced behind House, who was yelling, "This way!" as everyone bounded for the back of Norwood Boyd's house, scrambled up the back-porch steps, and stood at the back door, hearts pounding, pulses racing, eyes searching one another for *what's next?*

"Open it!" squealed Honey.

"Open it!" House called to Ben, indicating that his one good arm was full of dog and his other wasn't able to turn the doorknob.

The rain roared in their ears as they crowded like

frenzied cattle into the back kitchen. Gordon sobbed into Emma's chest.

"It's okay," said House. "We're safe in here. Safe."

The kitchen stretched the entire width of the back of the house. It was lined with windows on all three sides. Emma noticed the long counters and the tiny flowered tiles on the floor and the beams in the ceiling, the deep sink, the big old stove. It was family size, not industrial size, and it was perfect. *I could make hot dogs here*, thought Emma. *Baked beans. Cole slaw. Applesauce. And not one cake. Well, maybe just one cake at a time, like normal people do.*

"There's no electricity now," said House, "but I know where the flashlights are, if we need them."

He put down his dog and Honey embraced her, which made Gordon feel more at ease. He slipped out of Emma's arms and wiped his eyes with his hands. His tutu was crushed.

"YouDoggie," he said.

Emma handed House his baseball cap. He took it with a nod and a "Thanks." Emma nodded back.

Ruby blinked in the dim light and turned around as she looked, trying to take it all in.

"This way," said House. He pulled on his baseball cap. "I know this place."

"So you've said before," said Ruby. Her voice was the tiniest bit shaky as she followed House through the kitchen and down the wide hallway in the middle of the house. There was a love seat against the wall here, and a bureau there, and still the hallway seemed cavernous.

You could ride bikes in this hallway, thought Emma. *You could have picnics. Make forts.*

Spacious rooms opened on either side of the hallway as they walked—a pantry, a dining room, a study, a bedroom. At the end of the hall near the front door was another bedroom to the left and a living room to the right.

The parlor, thought Emma. *Of course there would be a parlor.*

It was paneled in a dark wood with bookcases lining the farthest wall.

There were substantial pieces of old furniture with names the children could not have known: a credenza, a steamer trunk, a camelback blanket chest. There were hanging tapestries, ginger and apothecary jars, jade trees, porcelain elephants, stone Buddhas, and books on the shelves, art on the walls, as well as an ornate Oriental carpet under their feet.

Emma kept her thoughts to herself. She stepped softly, she breathed softly, she thought softly. Her heart beat softly. *Swish-swish, swish-swish, swish-swish.* She kept her eyes wide open.

Eudora settled herself on a corner of the thick Oriental carpet near the great front windows and next to a long, carved table filled with games: clay marbles, metal jacks, etched checkers and a checkerboard, cards of all kinds, painted tops, elaborate mah-jongg tiles, and more. Honey and Gordon took off their shoes, shed their tutus, and chose some dominoes to play with on the wooden floor closest to the window light.

House pulled up the long, wooden blinds at the great front windows. Even with the rain pouring, there was plenty of white storm light from outside to illuminate the room and outline the contours of the life that had belonged to Norwood Boyd, age eighty-eight, philanthropist, philosopher, and maker of mystery.

"Good garden of peas," Ruby said.

"Whoa," said Ben.

Emma smiled. It was perfect.

THE AURORA COUNTY NEWS

HAPPENINGS IN HALLELUIA

SPECIAL-special edition
compiled and reported by
Phoebe "Scoop" Tolbert

I will be brief. I HAVE BREAKING NEWS.

As I was leaving the soiree for Dr. Dan this afternoon, right as the deluge of rain came upon us, I heard talk—I cannot reveal my sources, but we were all damp, and there went my hair—of a REVOLT about to take place at the Cake Café.

Customers will boycott the Grand Opening of the Cake Café (and Bakery) next week "or so" after reports from ... an unnamed source ... claiming that the pies at the Pine View (now made by the Cakes) are—suddenly—purposely not as good as Misanthrope Watkins's pies, and are in fact baked to be worse than Misanthrope's pies—on purpose!—in order to drive business AWAY from the Pine View and TO the Cake Café!

This reporter is so shocked by this news that she must go lie down with a cold cloth over her forehead. We've got Trouble! Right here in Halleluia! Right here in our perfect little town. Where's my fan?

Excuse me while I recuperate after filing this report. PT

(SEE? BRIEF.)

∽ Chapter Twenty-Eight ∽

They were seated comfortably—or as comfortably as they were going to get—on Norwood Boyd's old furniture. The couches and chairs had been covered in sheets, so House, one-handed, had pulled the sheets off, with Ben and Emma's help, and piled them in a spot near a red Chinese wedding chest.

"Sunshine Laundry, send us your sheets!" joked House, and Ruby couldn't believe it. She'd known House Jackson her entire life and had never heard him even try to be funny.

"Under new management," she rejoined. "Can't be beat!"

The laughter dispelled the collective strangeness and everybody found a seat. The sky had opened wide and the rain came down and down. It had been so thickly hot for so long; the humid summer air could not hold on to one more drop of moisture.

Dominoes clacked at the end of the room near the grand window, where Gordon and Honey worked in companionable silence, building a dotted house of their own. They were sleepy. Eudora Welty snored.

"I can't believe I'm sitting in this house," Ruby murmured. And then, when no one else spoke, Ruby added, "We're in for a good soaker. I hope the roof doesn't leak."

More silence. And then finally House spoke up.

"I can tell you a story while we wait."

The rain would come down for as long as it took, and the story would spin out for as long as House had breath; indeed he would tell it for as long as he lived.

And so he tugged at the brim of his baseball cap and began. He had been hired to read to the old man as he lay dying—Norwood's bedroom was across the wide hallway near the front door. Ruby shivered. House's elbow had been healing from its first injury—another story for another time—so he had read to Mr. Norwood instead of playing ball most of last year.

It took a lot longer for Mr. Norwood to die than House imagined it would, and he'd had to fight his own impulses to flee when he first started the job, because he, too, had heard the stories about how the house was haunted and held treasure, and how Mr. Norwood, who had closed himself up in this house years ago, was a monster, a baby-eater, and worse. But none of those stories was true.

Mr. Norwood had been a merchant marine for many years and had traveled the world collecting interesting memories and mementos. House gestured with his good hand around the room as if to say, *You can see, all these things from faraway places.*

"But then something happened to him," said House, "and I don't know what. He came home and closed himself up here and lived the rest of his life as a solitary. He had friends all over the world. They wrote to him and he wrote to them. He listened to music and tended a garden and took care of Eudora Welty—who was my mother's dog originally, though I don't remember any of that, because my mom died when I was six and Eudora already lived here then."

Emma blinked. Ben scratched at his ear. Ruby kept quiet. She knew about House's mother, and about Eudora Welty, and about Norwood Boyd, but being in his house, and listening to House tell the story, was another thing altogether.

House took a breath—it was a lot to tell anybody in one gulp, especially this special story. But he felt he was giving it into good hands, so he continued. "He read all the books on these shelves, and when he couldn't read to himself anymore, I started reading to him. We were reading *Treasure Island* when he died."

"The *moment* he died?" asked Ruby. She'd always wanted to know. House nodded. Ruby held her arms across her chest for safety. Ben and House exchanged a look. Ben's admiration for his friend grew as he listened.

Emma concentrated on the high ceilings and the sturdy walls and the solid wooden floors beneath her feet. She imagined four or five bedrooms upstairs. Hers would be in the turret.

I'm here, she told the old abandoned house. And she sent

those words to Norwood Boyd as well. *Here I am. Do you want a girl to love your house? I do.*

"Who took care of Norwood?" asked Ruby. "If he couldn't even hold a book to read, how did he eat? Or do anything else?"

"Mr. Pip came by every day," said House. "Or Miss Mattie. And probably others. My dad, for one. He had friends, even if he didn't venture out in the world."

"What about the house?" asked Emma.

"Norwood built the house himself," said House. "A long time ago."

"It's a big house for one person," said Ruby, "and it doesn't look anything like all the other houses around here. Why did he need such a big house?"

"Maybe he didn't think he would end up alone," whispered Emma. "Maybe he filled it with treasures for the family he never had."

"That's too sad to even think about," said Ruby. "And creepy."

"It's not creepy at all," said Emma.

"How do you know?" asked Ruby. "You didn't even know him."

"Neither did you!" said Emma.

Ben changed the subject. "It's a *great* house!"

House smiled. None of the All-Stars had thought it was a great house. Of course. But Ben wasn't burdened by the rumors, the myths, the prejudices, the fears. It *was* a great house.

Emma tried not to speak of her excitement, not to show it, but when Ben declared this a great house, she couldn't contain herself and burst out with, "It's mine!"

~ Chapter Twenty-Nine ~

Emma clapped her hand over her mouth and looked at Ben, wide-eyed. In an instant, she could tell he had been thinking the very same thing.

Ruby pursed her lips and said nothing. They were birdbrains, these two. Who would want a once-haunted, dilapidated house?

"I don't know who it belongs to now," said House. "Or what's going to happen to it." He said it as smoothly as if it had been no big deal for Emma to burst out with her ownership of it.

"Who hired you to read to Mr. Norwood?" asked Ruby, bringing the story back to the center of the conversation.

"It was Mr. Pip."

"Pip!" Ruby sat up straight and pushed her hair out of her face. "Mr. Pip?"

"He and Norwood were best friends," said House. "They were best friends when they were kids, and kept on being best friends until the end."

Would he tell them the rest? He would. "There's a picture out there in the hallway of Pip wearing Mr. Norwood's baseball uniform, when they were both twelve years old—a long time ago."

Ruby slid off the couch. "Let me see it."

House got a flashlight from the table next to the hallway and said, "Come on." Honey and Gordon had succumbed to the sound of the rain and were both sleeping on the rug next to the snoring Eudora Welty. They had had quite the fright, and it was perfect napping weather.

Emma, Ben, House, and Ruby trooped out to the hallway. The walls were packed with framed photos of all sizes, the story of a life.

The rain slowed to a drizzle and the sun began to glide through the front window. A shaft of light shone on the hallway, just where Parting Schotz stood, frozen in time in his picture frame, smiling all over his twelve-year-old face, wearing a uniform that said AURORA ANGELS on it.

"Why is he wearing Norwood's uniform instead of his own?" asked Ruby.

"It's a long story," said House. "Pip told it to me after Norwood died."

"What's the short version?"

House shoved the brim of his baseball cap right, left, then back to center. "Pip couldn't play with the white boys, on their team, when they were kids, and Mr. Norwood quit the team when he found out. Then neither one of them played ball. And they were both real good ballplayers."

"Good garden of peas," said Ruby. "I never knew this story."

"Neither did I," said House. "Pip told me that Norwood was a catcher, and could throw a ball clean from home to second base to get a batter out."

"I'm a catcher!" said Ruby.

"What about Mr. Pip?" asked Ben.

"Pip was the best hitter Norwood had ever seen. And you should have seen him at our All-Stars game! He knocked one out of the park and he's eighty-eight years old! He saved the game!"

"He did," confirmed Ruby.

Ben softly whistled his admiration. "Wish I'd seen that."

There was silence then—a contemplation of those two twelve-year-old boys and their friendship. Ruby began to reevaluate her opinion of House Jackson. Actually, she'd never thought much about House at all. Maybe she had dismissed him because he was—until today—so quiet, or because he was such good friends with that Cleebo Wilson who drove her nuts with his bravado and bragging.

Ruby watched House lift his baseball cap and resettle it on his forehead. His face was red, the way people's faces color up when they've said things that are important to them to say. He was cute.

She shook her head. She course-corrected. "We should

go. The storm's over." She looked up and down the hall-way. "Where's Emma?"

They found her outside at the garden fence, her practical side already hard at work, moving forward. It was one thing to decide a house belonged to you. It was quite another to make it a reality. First things first. Her father had to decide to stay.

"Can we really make a garden out of this mess?" she asked.

"We can if we chop the weeds and bring in my chick-ens," said Ruby.

"How will you get them all the way over here?" asked Ben.

Ruby sniffed at Mr. Nitpick and said, "Mr. Butterfield has a chicken tractor. It's really an old school bus he turned into a portable chicken coop. You use 'em for mov-ing your chickens from place to place, so they can have new grass all the time. He'll haul 'em over for us, I bet. And they can stay until they've finished the job. We'll look after them every day."

"Everybody will know we're here if we tell somebody else!" said Emma. "My dad can say no before we even get started!"

Ruby thought about it. "Miss Eula can do it for us. We'll have to tell her our plan. And she'll have to tell Mr. Butterfield, but he won't tell anybody else. He's a lawyer, and he can't talk about other people's business. So nobody else will know the plan."

Honey, Gordon, and Eudora Welty appeared on the back porch, half-awake. "Where did everybody go?"

Emma agreed about Miss Eula. "Can we start tomorrow?" she asked.

And so it was decided.

~ Chapter Thirty ~

Back at the Cake Café, Leo and Arlouin had baked a batch of Comfort Cookies. They were still wearing their aprons and their somber moods. The radio played softly in the kitchen. "Who's Sorry Now" wafted into the front room. The CLOSED sign was on the door, as it was every afternoon, and the two Cakes sat at their favorite wooden table near the glass bakery case, where they liked to admire their work. But they weren't in an admiring mood this late afternoon after the soiree.

Leo was shaken that Parting Schotz would know his father's name, but his nerves settled as he told himself that anyone could find out about Archibald Cake just by asking about the Cakes themselves. Leo had told the story of Archie to five or six—or was it fifteen or twenty?—customers who asked where the Cakes were from, and any of them—all of them—would surely have mentioned the story to Pip. One thing a body could be sure of in this town was gossip.

And beyond that, Pip was an old man; old people mixed things up. Especially if they'd been knocked in the head like that.

So Leo soothed himself and didn't mention his under-the-table conversation with Pip to Arlouin. He was sure he'd never been to Halleluia, Mississippi, even though the place felt familiar in a way he couldn't articulate.

"Cakes never go anywhere twice!" Archie had told his young son, his only child, Leo. "We do our best and we move on. There is so much need in the world, after all, and cake is one simple way to soothe it."

The dogs had heaped themselves at Leo's and Arlouin's feet. "They need comfort, too," said Leo. He fed them a cookie apiece.

"Bad dogs," said Arlouin, but she said it with great affection. The song on the radio changed and "I Fall to Pieces" drifted to them as they sat and sighed and munched.

Dot Land, Halleluia's postmistress, opened the café door and called "Yoo-hoo!" and waltzed in with a bushel basket of mail. "I've been looking for you!" she said. "When your boys came in yesterday to check, we didn't have your forwarded mail yet, but"—she raised the basket high over her head—"here it is!"

"Come in, Dot," said a weary Arlouin. "Have a Comfort Cookie."

"Oh, no, thank you," said Dot in a warm but firm voice. She had a pearl-handled comb peacocked in her short natural hair. "I am watching my waistline."

"Do you expect it to run off?" asked Leo in his own weary voice, making a bad joke and laughing at it ruefully in spite of himself.

Bo-Bo gave Dot a kiss as Dot helped herself to a seat at the wooden table with the plate of cookies.

"Look, you two." Dot put the mail basket in her lap. "It's okay. Nobody blames you or your dogs for crashing the party. It could have happened to anyone."

"It was pandemonium," said Leo. "A pandemonium *bonanza*. How do you know about it?"

"You think I don't know everything that goes on in this town?" said Dot. "I'm postmistress!"

"Well, you didn't see it," said Leo. He took a bite of cookie.

"I couldn't leave work!" said Dot.

"Finesse screamed at my children," said Arlouin. "She scared them away! And she said that our family ruined everything." Arlouin ate another Comfort Cookie.

"Well, that's the pot calling the kettle black," declared Dot. "I remember when Finesse—*Frances*—broke House's arm in that same barbershop a year ago, and ruined his baseball summer, and almost lost them the All-Stars game this year, to boot! She'll come around; don't worry about her. And your kids will come home, too. They can't have gone far."

"Gordon went to Honey's with House," said Arlouin.

"See, there you go."

"I'm sure Ben will be there, too," Arlouin continued. "And that means Emma is with Ruby."

"Have a cookie, Dot," said Leo. "Please."

Dot helped herself to a cookie, took a bite, closed her eyes, and sighed with pleasure. It was a good cookie. The rain had slowed to pitter-patters on the tin roof above them. The boys were upstairs playing something that involved lots of rolling around and laughing and bumping into things, with occasional shouting and catapulting off the top bunk beds. A normal rainy afternoon's fun.

"Maybe it will be all right," Arlouin hoped.

"Of course it will be all right," said Dot. "And look at all this mail I've brought you! I'll bet there's something in here to lift your spirits."

"Thank you, Dot," said Leo with feeling. "You lift our spirits, too."

Dot took another bite of cookie. "I'm telling you, I've never seen a body in this town get so much mail from such far-flung places!"

"We do get mail from all over," agreed Arlouin.

"Well," continued Dot, "except for Norwood Boyd, who could have been a stamp collector with all the exotic stamps that came affixed to his letters! Postmarks from the Philippines, Madagascar, Australia, Guam, India—and that's just for starters! He traveled so much as a young man and he had so many friends, wrote so many letters, got so much mail . . ."

"Who?" asked Leo.

"Norwood Boyd," said Dot, blushing a little at her crowing. She loved to talk about the mail. "Nobody has mail home delivery here, as you know, but Norwood was different, and Carl Fontana—you know him, our deputy postmaster—he delivered Norwood's mail once a week and picked up and mailed his replies as well."

"Have I met him?" asked Leo.

"Carl Fontana?" Dot adjusted the comb in her hair.

"No," said Leo. "Norwood Boyd. I know that name. I think I've met him!"

"I should say not," said Dot. She eyed the cookie plate. "Norwood died, poor soul, before you arrived in Halleluia."

"Oh," said Leo. "I misunderstood."

"I'm so sorry to hear it," added Arlouin. She held up the cookie plate for Dot.

"Well, he lived a long life," said Dot, taking another cookie. "And he was a friend to all who knew him." She rose and put the mail basket on her chair. "I've got to go," she said. "Enjoy your mail call!" She smiled and left the café holding another cookie, or maybe it was two cookies, or maybe it was a napkin full of cookies. Dot departed with cookies.

Leo pushed up the nose of his glasses and looked at Arlouin. "That name is so familiar."

"Norwood Boyd?"

"Yes. No. I don't remember."

"Rain's stopped!" yelled the Cake boys as they tumbled over one another down the stairs and out the back door. The rain had scoured the sandy lane to a shine. Pumpkin-colored pebbles gleamed in the sunlight, warm and wet and washed. The boys left the back door open and the dogs followed them outside.

"Norwood Boyd?" Arlouin repeated, as she got up to shut the door and turn on the overhead fan.

But Leo had pushed the thought aside, like he pushed all reflection aside. He was not a ruminating man. He lived in the moment with one eye to the future, where nothing was spoiled and everything was possible and there lived an eternal beginning.

"Let's see what the mail brought," he said.

Even though they had moved many times in the past twelve years, the Cakes had had only one address, a central mailbox where all their correspondence was sent. It had been the same address all during Leo Cake's childhood as well—the only address he'd ever known.

Anyone who wanted to send mail to the Cakes had been sending it there for ages. Every so often, when he remembered, Leo directed the mail place to send the accumulated mail and it was forwarded. Then Leo sifted through the thank-you letters and the bills and the requests for help.

What would we have done without you? Your William Tell's Never-Miss Apple Cake saved the day! Love, Vinnie and Vaughn and the boys.

"Was that in Amarillo or Plano?" asked Leo.

"Austin," said Arlouin. She folded each letter and put it back in its envelope as Leo opened the next.

You changed our lives for the better with your Grilled Tortilla and Onion Cakes with Nuts and Caramel Frosting! Muchas Gracias! Love, Jorge and Louisa and everyone at the Hatch Chile Farm.

"Was that New Haven or New York?"

"Neither," said Arlouin.

We'll never forget you! Hungarian Plum Cakes forever! Love, George and Louisa at Evergreen Farms.

"Was that North Dakota or South Dakota?

"Honestly, Leo."

Word of mouth brought the requests.

"This one looks promising," said Leo. "An old family bakery burned down in Sesquidilla, California, and nobody bakes there."

"Nobody?"

"They don't even cook! They need us right away!"

"Was anyone hurt?"

"Just the buns!" Leo laughed too hard at his own joke. Arlouin smacked him on the shoulder with an empty envelope. "Stop that! This is a tragedy!"

"Which is why we should go help them," said Leo, suddenly somber. "Everything up in smoke." He rubbed his chin with the backs of his fingers. "Disaster is what happens when you stay somewhere too long. You accumulate too many things. And then, when something bad happens, you lose everything. Or everything is a mess. Ugly. Imperfect. Old. Broken."

"That's not true, Leo," said Arlouin. "What happens when you stay somewhere a long time is you have long, deep friendships with history and texture and meaning . . . and you watch the people you love become old . . . and you become old with them . . ." She trailed off, lost in her thoughts, which were also, she was discovering, her wishes. "You get to know a place."

"I know this place well enough already," said Leo in his weariest voice.

"It's not time to move yet," continued Arlouin. "You said yourself, weather patterns are stable right now."

"There's been a big rain," said Leo. "It has brought in a new front, which can serve as a providential sign. It's best to travel when the weather signs are fortuitous. We should have a place picked out, just in case, before we go."

Arlouin reached across the table and took her husband's hand. "Leo, these people in California. They have people. They have friends and families—an entire community—who will help them."

"We're almost done here, Arlouin, really we are. The Pine View is perking along, and Misanthrope has taught us all she knows about piecrust, and surely someone else will come along soon who can take over for us in the pie-making department."

As Leo finished his sentence, Miss Mattie Perkins stormed into the café. She slammed the door behind her. Arlouin and Leo both jumped in their chairs.

Miss Mattie was furious. "Well, don't just sit there!" she snapped.

∽ Chapter Thirty-One ∽

"Mattie!" said Leo and Arlouin together.

"I'll take ten of those applesauce muffins," said Miss Mattie. "Not that anyone will buy them. What's wrong with this town?"

"What's the matter, Mattie?" Arlouin felt her face drain of color.

"There's a boycott!" spit Miss Mattie. "You don't know? You haven't heard? A ridiculous, idiotic boycott!"

"Of what?" asked Leo, rising from his chair.

"Of you!" said Miss Mattie. Mary Wilson opened the door and, in her haste to get to her friends, left it wide open. "Are y'all okay in here?" she asked, anxious. "I just heard."

"Why is there a boycott?" Arlouin asked. She stood up and removed her apron.

"It's your pies," said Miss Mattie. "They don't taste like Misanthrope's and they used to, and everyone can tell, and someone is afraid you're trying to run him out of business. Someone idiotic. Pie is pie."

"What?" Leo heard, but he didn't understand.

"I can make a pie that ordinary at home," said Clemmie Watson. She stood in the open doorway of the Cake Café. "I don't need to go to the Pine View for it."

"For heaven's sake, Clementine," said Miss Mattie, "it's pie!"

"It's not Misanthrope's pie," sniffed Clementine. She walked on.

Arlouin blinked at Miss Mattie. "I don't know what to say."

"Well, I do," said Leo. "Those pies tasted like Misanthrope's pies for the first week because they *were* Misanthrope's pies. She was in our kitchen! She taught us how to make them! Her crust is especially tricky, but we think we mastered it. What's the problem?"

"The problem is not you," said Miss Mattie. "Ten muffins, please."

The bottomless muffin basket suddenly held no muffins. It was a sad basket. "I could have sworn I filled it this morning," said Arlouin.

"You don't have to sell our muffins at your store, Mattie." Leo took off his apron and pushed up his glasses. "Let me go talk to Jerome and settle this. No one is trying to drive business away from the Pine View. We came to help!"

"We are not pie people," said Arlouin softly. "We are Cakes."

"Suit yourself," Miss Mattie said. "But I will gladly put some muffins at my register, in solidarity. I'm sure Dot Land will put some on the counter at the post office, and

Pip will take a dozen at the barbershop. There *are* sane people in this town."

"I'll take at least a dozen," said Mary Wilson. "And I'll make sure they sell! I'll make a sign: *It's Time for Breakfast in Bed! Then Send Us Your Sheets!*"

"Let me know if you change your mind," said Miss Mattie.

Miss Mattie and Mary Wilson swept out the door and Leo Cake locked it behind them. Enough visitors. Enough of everything. The Pine View was closed for the day, too. He would have to talk with Jerome in the morning.

"We've never been in competition in a town before," Arlouin said. "I did think that was strange when we moved here."

"Yes," said Leo. "I did, too. It's not what we usually do, or how we usually work. Still, we serve a mostly breakfast crowd, while the Pine View does a huge midday meal every day. We just serve some soup and sandwiches at lunch."

"And cake," reminded Arlouin.

"And cake," said Leo.

The back door slammed open, and Van raced inside.

"We're boycotted!" he yelled. He waved a flyer like a flag and shoved it into Arlouin's hands as he ran back out the door yelling, "What's boycotted?"

"Feed the dogs!" Arlouin hollered after him.

Leo took the flyer from Arlouin's hand and read it. "Look at this," he said, his voice laced with despair.

Arlouin read it out loud.

All customers who eat at the Pine View are asked to boycott the Cake Café, as they have been purposely making substandard pies for us in an effort to steal our beloved diners. In addition to the boycott, anyone interested in taking over for Misanthrope Watkins in the Pie Department is asked to report to the kitchen of the Pine View for a pie-making and tasting tryout tomorrow at four a.m.—YES, A.M.—when we open to audition pie chefs. Tasting to commence at six a.m. All are welcome.

"Four a.m.!" was all Arlouin could think to say.

"I got it wrong," said Leo. He flopped back into his chair and Arlouin sat down again as well. "We weren't meant to come here." Leo took off his glasses and began to clean them with his apron.

Arlouin read the note again, to herself. Then she looked around the café at all their hard work, all the time they had invested in making themselves a place in this new town.

"You never showed me the letter that made you decide to move us here," she said.

"I told you about it," said Leo.

"That's not the same," said Arlouin. "You said it was compelling. That tells me nothing."

"People here are right," repeated Leo. "This town does not need two cafés. This town does not *deserve* two cafés. Why did I ever think it was a good idea to come here?"

"Yes!" said Arlouin. "Why did you! Why, Leo? Why?"

Leo took a deep breath and let it out in a long, slow exhale. He walked into the industrial kitchen, picked up a canister of baking powder, and brought it back to the little wooden table, where he opened it and took out a handwritten note. He shook off the excess leavening and handed it to his wife.

In a beautiful, flowing script was written two words:

Come Now.

~ *Chapter Thirty-Two* ~

Six children and one old dog were having the time of their lives in a weedy old garden, in a neglected old yard, near a dilapidated old house, protected by benevolent old trees, in a venerable old woods.

Ben stalked into the nearby forest and introduced House to the sport of peeing contests, because Gordon couldn't wait for a bathroom. Gordon was giddy to be included with the big boys.

Emma and Ruby and Honey found treasures in the overgrown garden. A trowel, a shovel, a watering can, a plate, a pair of gloves, and a bunch of old bricks and stones that marked paths long ago.

"Here's a volunteer tomato!" yelled Ruby. "You're in such luck!" It was flowering but had not set fruit yet. Ruby marked it with a tall stick. "We'll keep the chickens away from it with a little chicken wire," she said. "Here's some more!"

It was easy to pull up weeds after the rain, and soon they had piles where they stood. Emma's muscled eleven-year-old arms would be useful in a garden. She was proud of that.

House retrieved Honey's and Gordon's tutus and brought bottles of water from the pantry in Mr. Norwood's house, bottles that Pip or Miss Mattie had brought. Everyone sat on the back steps and had a drink. Eudora drank from the old garden plate.

While House and Ben talked baseball, Emma remembered her index cards and pulled them out of her pocket. She borrowed Ruby's pencil, turned over the card that read *Ben has a terrible imagination*, and drew a plan for her new turret room. On another card she drew a picture of the upstairs of the house and assigned bedrooms to her brothers. She even designed a bathroom with a deep tub for her mother's soaking baths. Never mind that she hadn't seen the upstairs of the house. Her imagination filled in the gaps.

Ruby pulled her reconnaissance list out of her overalls pocket. "I can see we need to make adjustments." She took her pencil from Emma.

"The chickens will dig up that garden in no time flat. You'll be ready to plant beans, at least, this summer, and all kinds of fall crops, like peas and greens and beets and carrots—even potatoes."

Emma wondered how Ruby could know so much about gardening, in such detail, and then she realized Ruby was reading from a list her mother had given her.

"It might look something like this," Ruby said as she turned over the reconnaissance list to draw on the back of it, "although I'm no artist."

"Oh, that looks *fine*," said Emma in a satisfied, happy

voice. She had no idea what she was looking at, but it had rows and words on the rows and that was enough.

"There's compost over here!" shouted Ben. He'd wandered to the far side of the garden fence. "It hasn't been touched in a long time, but it's full of good dirt and a ton of worms!"

"Look who's a compost expert, all of a sudden!" Ruby shouted back. That boy.

"You would be, too, if you had Miss Mattie standing over you while you turned compost," said Ben. This girl.

"Do you think it's okay, House, to make a garden here?" asked Emma. She really, really wanted it to be okay.

"It's not for me to say," replied House, "but as long as you don't damage anything, I don't think Mr. Norwood would mind. He might like it that the garden was being used. Tell me again why you want to grow a garden?"

"So she doesn't have to move," said Ruby in her *isn't it obvious* voice.

It wasn't obvious.

"I want it to be a secret," said Emma. "I want to get it just perfect and then tell my dad. If the garden is planted and we're getting beans and peas and tomatoes for soups—"

"It's past time for planting new tomatoes," interrupted Ruby. "You can plant tomatoes and corn and okra and squash and peppers next year."

Emma was fine with that, too. She was giddy with possibility. And by next year, they might be living in this wonderful house! It *spoke* to her, she was sure of it. It *needed* her. There was no doubt, none at all. And when her father saw the truth of it—the garden, the house, and Emma's permanent plan—well, he wouldn't want to leave again, ever. After all, she was *giving* him a house.

Ben offered to carry the sleepy Honey home and House accepted the help. The boys walked off with Honey and Eudora in one direction, and the girls took Gordon and walked in the other. The woods were darkening with the day and they wanted to get out of them quickly, but they didn't tramp through the forest the way they had when Ben first led them to Emma's magical house. They walked out through the big iron gates and down the orange-pebbled driveway and along the dirt road into town.

"We really need to get started," said Ruby. "It's already July. I'll ask Miss Eula to help us tonight."

Emma nodded. "I can't help until we finish the lunch rush tomorrow. We bake pies for the Pine View before it's even sunrise, and then cakes, and bread, and soup at the same time. I have to help."

"I'll leave you a note in our tree tonight," said Ruby. "I'll let you know what Miss Eula says."

Our tree. Emma almost hugged herself. *Our garden. Our*

house. In her imagination she was already moved in and rolling her Friend Atlas across the wall of her turret room, securing it to those turret walls forever, writing to all of her old friends to tell them about her new home, her new address, her permanent place in the world, and inviting them all to come visit.

~ Chapter Thirty-Three ~

" 'Come Now'?" read Arlouin. "Who wrote this, Leo?"

"I don't know!" said Leo Cake. "And I don't know why I answered it, Arlouin. Honestly, I thought I was replying to the letter asking us to help start a teaching bakery in a downtown elementary school with one thousand students!"

"Well, we're obviously not doing that," said Arlouin.

"Obviously not," Leo agreed. "But the envelopes were similar—both of them yellow—and I think I wrote back using the wrong address."

Arlouin licked her lips. "Or maybe you did mean to come here," she said. "I mean, you hid the letter in the baking powder canister! You said this place felt familiar. You thought Norwood Boyd's name was familiar. Honestly, Leo. What's going on?"

Leo slid his hands up and down his face. His glasses swept to the top of his head and stayed there. "Maybe you're right," he said. "I was startled when I saw that handwriting, and I thought it looked familiar, and I think I had a gut reaction and answered that letter, even though—you know me—so many things look familiar to me, Arlouin, and here we came, in answer to *Come Now*, but nothing has happened by our coming now. I think I made a mistake!"

"So now what do we do?"

Leo reached for the pile of mail on the table, held it up, and let it fall dramatically through his fingers. Twice. It was a lot of mail. "All these people really need help!"

"Leo . . ." began Arlouin.

"No!" he said. "Coming here *was* a mistake. I see that now. And we haven't been here long. We can fix this, and fix it quickly. I'm going to go next door before the post office closes and send an overnight letter to these California bakery people."

"What?"

"That's what we're going to do. We're going to go where we're needed. Where there aren't boycotts and naysayers and competition. Call in the kids. We leave in the morning!"

～ Chapter Thirty-Four ～

Emma left Gordon on the ball field with the boys and raced across the sandy lane to the back of the café. She threw open the red door just as her mother opened it from the other side.

"Emma!" Arlouin said in surprise.

"No time to talk!" Emma gasped. She took the stairs two at a time and ran into her tiny room at the back of the house, slammed the door, took her index cards out of her shorts pocket, and pinned them with Ruby's red pin to her Friend Atlas. "There!" she said. "It's real!" Ruby's picture fluttered to the floor.

Emma rummaged at her desk for more pins. She pinned Ruby back on her atlas, took a fresh index card, and wrote on it, in red colored pencil:

Ruby Lavender, age 11
Halleluia, Mississippi

Good idea person.
Terrible with details.
Loud. Impulsive. Means well.
Persistent bordering on pushy.

She thought for a moment with her pencil between her teeth and added:

> Forgave me when I told Ben one of
> our secrets.
> Secretly thinks Ben is cute.
> Might think House is cute. (He is.)

And then:

> Loyal
> Honest
> Hard-working
> (not calm)

She heard a commotion outside and opened her window to see what was happening. The dusky night was filled with lightning bugs just beginning their glowing dances. She had missed dinner. Maybe they all had.

"What's happening down there?!" she called. She felt like Ebenezer Scrooge calling down to the young boy, *What day is it? Have I missed it?* in *A Christmas Carol*, when he wakes up on Christmas morning to find out that the long night and the endless journey has been only a dream, and a new life awaits him. Starting now. Heavens! Where was that practical, reasonable, give-me-the-facts girl? She didn't feel practical at all anymore. She felt . . .

"We're moving!" shouted Jody and Van and Roger. Their voices were full of anguish. They were sobbing. They didn't even try to hide their despair.

And the dogs. They drooped and sloped and rambled and swayed like they were on their last legs. Maybe they were.

Arlouin had Gordon in her arms. She looked besieged.

Gordon flailed and howled like the world was coming to an end.

And that's because it was.

⌒ Chapter Thirty-Five ⌒

Packing. Again.

All around Emma, boxes were being filled. Some had never been emptied. The upstairs kitchen, where Emma had first met Ruby Lavender, was once again full of taped boxes.

"The movers will be here in two days," said Leo. "Let's have everything shipshape for them to move us. We'll be driving through Colorado by then. Who has seen my road atlas?"

No one spoke more than was necessary. The boys silently gathered their bicycles and packed their suitcases and had no energy for arguments. Arlouin was tight-lipped as she set out leftovers for supper. There was still pimento cheese, and day-old bread, and a soup Emma had experimented with earlier in the week, a Cold Cucumber Soup with Yogurt and Dill and Homemade Croutons. It was delicious but the boys wouldn't touch it. Arlouin unearthed the peanut butter and jelly for them.

Ben arrived home to packing boxes.

"What! Again? Already? What's happening?"

Now, thought Emma. *Finally Ben gets it.* But her heartbreak was so deep she couldn't speak. She couldn't be in the same room as her father. She couldn't begin to explain it to her mother. She couldn't even look at her oldest brother. They had shared something important earlier that day, and now it was gone. Forever. She walked upstairs and closed her bedroom door.

Now, thought Ben. *Now I see why Emma hates it so much.* But no amount of cajoling or explaining or questioning his father changed anything. They were leaving.

"We go when it's time," said his mother, without conviction. "You know that."

"Good," his father had said when he saw his son. "You're here. Give me a hand loading the car, will you?"

The Ford Econoline took on more and more weight and changed its shape as box after suitcase after bicycle was strapped to its luggage and bicycle racks front and back.

Into the night they packed and readied themselves to go.

No one turned on the radio.

"We leave at first light," said Leo.

Emma kept checking her tree every time she walked out to the car with a box, a book, a tin of cookies for them to eat on their journey. The knothole was always empty. She put her hand on the cold, smooth trunk and felt no rough pulse, no smile, no warmth.

Finally, the Cakes called it a night. Leo and Arlouin disappeared into their front bedroom after their good-nights. The boys would not allow their parents to kiss them and began to cry again.

Gordon, who had slept on a pallet for weeks and had been so proud of it he had sung every night at bedtime the song his mother taught him, "Make Me a Pallet on Your Floor," squished into bed with Roger. Roger moved over wordlessly to welcome him.

Ben tried to talk to Emma. She was in her bedroom, sitting on her bed and staring at her Friend Atlas.

"I'm sorry about the house," he said. "I know you loved it."

Emma turned her face to Ben. It held no trace of emotion or recognition. It was as if Ben were a stranger speaking in a tongue Emma didn't understand. She blinked and stared back at her atlas.

"Well . . ." said Ben, not knowing what to say next, "I'll see you in the morning. You can have my spot in the car, if you want it. It's the best one." When Emma didn't answer, Ben left his sister and walked into the living-room bedroom to think his own sad thoughts and fall asleep with his brothers.

Outside Emma's open window a melancholic breeze dusted up from the sandy lane, the ball fields, the dirt roads around town, the woods paths, and even the paved Main Street that went through the heart of Halleluia, Mississippi. It was searching for someone or something.

The rain had cooled the earth. The front that came in with the rain spooned up tiny tendrils of fog left over from the steaming of the day.

But Emma didn't see any of that. She only saw her Friend Atlas and the long succession of moves and more moves she had made and would make, for the rest of her life.

She could not bear to hold on to her hope anymore. She could not bear to risk her heart, ever again. And she could not bear to remember.

So she picked up the heavy black-handled scissors on her desk.

She cut her Friend Atlas to pieces.

~ Chapter Thirty-Six ~

Emma was still awake at midnight when she heard a clanging and got up to investigate. She tiptoed down the stairs, toward the light in the industrial kitchen, and found her mother up to her arms in cake batter.

Arlouin blew a stray lock of hair from her face and said, "I'm making a Grand Closing Cake. Want to help me?"

This was new. Emma put on her apron.

In silence they chopped the dates and grated the coconut and rolled the seeds and toasted the nuts and melted the butter and whisked the eggs and measured the milk and flour and soda and sugar and salt and vanilla, and stirred the batter by hand instead of using the giant mixer. The metallic oven ticked its companionable heating-up *tap-tap-tap* as the room filled with the comforting sounds and sights and smells of what the Cakes did best.

There was no recipe for this cake. Arlouin used what she had on hand and improvised. The fundamental mechanics of cake have been the same since the dawn of cakes. A grain, a leavening, a fat, a liquid, a binding agent, flavorings, air, heat, cooling. Baking is chemistry as an art form, and the Cakes had mastered it.

They were mesmerized by it as well. Cake was different every time it was baked. It had so many iterations but was fundamentally the same thing, day after day, time after time, cake after cake.

"I'm sorry, Emma," said Arlouin as they shoved a full-sheet cake pan—enough cake to feed a hundred people, their biggest cake pan—into the gaping mouth of their widest oven.

Emma began to fill the sink with soapy water while her mother wiped down counters. When she finally felt she could risk a few words without crying, she said, "Why, Mom? Why do we always go?"

Arlouin started to give her daughter the stock family answer, *We suit up and we show up*, but then she changed her mind. She brought her dishrag to the sink and rinsed it, began to wipe more counter, and admitted, "I don't know anymore, Emma."

Emma turned off the water. "There's this house," she began. "And a garden . . ."

Arlouin shook her head. "You know what your father says about houses."

Emma turned to her mother. "No, I don't. What does he say?"

Arlouin checked on her cake through the window at the oven door. "He always says, 'We'll have a house of our own someday, Arlouin, when we aren't needed elsewhere.'"

"When will we stop being needed elsewhere?" Emma felt the tears. This would not do.

"That's a good question," said Arlouin.

"I haven't even had the chance to say good-bye to my friends." The tears were going to come.

"I know," said Arlouin. "I wish there was time."

Arlouin embraced her daughter, and Emma buried her face in her mother's shoulder, but she steadfastly refused to cry. The cake baked. The breeze shifted. The world ticked on in time.

As the cake came out of the oven and cooled, Arlouin and Emma made chocolate frosting, did the dishes, then iced their Grand Closing Cake and dusted it with confectioners' sugar.

It was beautiful.

Emma would not check the knothole again. There hadn't been a note at ten p.m. or eleven p.m. or twelve a.m. or one a.m. Finding a note would hurt as much as not having one. She was done with that tree and with impulsive decisions, not to mention impetuous hope.

"Let's get some sleep," said Arlouin. She sighed softly. "Tomorrow we'll have a long drive."

They left their beautiful cake on the prep table in the industrial kitchen, turned out the lights, followed each other up the stairs, and finally climbed into their beds.

It was four a.m.

The lights clicked on across Main Street, at the Pine View Café.

SPECIAL TO THE AURORA COUNTY NEWS

HAPPENINGS IN HALLELUIA

You-Won't-Believe-This Edition!

compiled and reported by

Phoebe "Scoop" Tolbert

This reporter was so shocked to receive a boycott flyer on her front porch yesterday that she rose at three a.m. this morning, dashed to the Pine View Café at four a.m., and forgot to take off her bobby-pinned-toilet-paper hat (excuse me, bobby-pinned-TP hat) that she wears on the back of her head at night to make sure she doesn't wreck her Aquanetted hairdo.

You cannot imagine how different we all look at four a.m., but that is another story for another column. Suffice it to say that, as I arrived, Jonetta James took me aside and helped my hair out of its bobby-pinned prison. I put my carefully constructed TP hat in my pocketbook and took out my notebook so I could report to readers from a bird's-eye point of view the dramatic—

PIE-OFF AT THE PINE VIEW.

You're welcome.

Three Pie Contestants showed up at the Pine View: the aforementioned Jonetta James (who confessed to me that she really didn't want the job, she just wanted out of the house), Luther Ray Vandross, and—you will not believe it, dear reader—Cornelia Ishee, known colloquially, locally as Aunt Tot.

What you further will not believe is that Tot Ishee *will be* the new Pie Chef at the Pine View Café! I had to pull out my smelling salts at this news, but I must confess that one (hesitant!) taste of her piecrust was enough to convince me that some people just have to find the right venue for their talents and then they can soar.

(Much like the way my talent is soaring! Thank you for writing in, readers, and thank you for the extra space, Editor Johnson.)

Tot will *not* be making the pie *fillings*, it must be noted, as her fillings were inedible. (I'm so sorry to be so blunt, but this is a reporter's job, you will understand.)

The pie-filling job will go to Luther Ray Vandross! His coconut cream was a dream, his chocolate cream was the creamiest, and his lemon meringue made our tongues twirl. "I have plans for a banana cream as well!" he declared.

Jerome Fountainbleu was beside himself. "Better than ever!" he crowed. "We are better than ever at the Pine View!"

"But how on earth?" was the shared sentiment of the pie testers who had arrived in droves at six a.m. for the taste testing. "How on earth . . . Tot Ishee?"

Misanthrope Watkins educated us:

"There is an energy that flows from a baker's heart through her arms and hands and fingers. It informs the dough. Anyone can measure and mix, but no one can replace your passion, your perfect-to-you energy, and the knowing that comes from years of practice. Tot Ishee has had years of cooking practice, this is true. She just didn't know until today that her energy is a perfect match for piecrust."

Tot Ishee beamed, I tell you. *Beamed.* If you had stared at her too hard, her smile would have singed your retinas.

"Furthermore," Misanthrope continued, "I made those pies for the Cakes, in the first week they were here, in order to show them how to do it. Then the Cakes took over. And, well . . . as heavenly as they are at cakes, they are just not pie people. It wasn't for lack of trying! They did their best! And they were not trying to siphon customers from the Pine View. They were doing us a service until we could find someone better."

Misanthrope glared at Jerome Fountainbleu, who mumbled something about having to take out the trash as he slunk out of the kitchen.

Miss Mattie Perkins appeared at this point— doesn't she always appear at *the* crucial moment? (I asked her this question and she snapped, "I always come into town early to open my store, Phoebe!") Mattie bristled at everyone that they should be ashamed of themselves for spreading such malicious gossip about perfectly pleasant people.

"You owe them an apology," she fumed. "Put *that* on a flyer." Well!

I do apologize, dear readers. I *am* ashamed of myself for spreading such malodorous gossip in this very column. But wait. No, I'm not. But I want to be. I am hosting Pastor Merson for dinner this week, and we shall discuss it.

In the meantime, we have had the mistiest weather this morning. An insistent little fog has found its way into my French twist updo. I must go re-pin my hair in its TP tent and get my beauty rest. I shall even take the phone off the hook. *That's* how serious I am about taking good care of myself. You should be, too.

Yours Faithfully, PT

~ Chapter Thirty-Seven ~

A soft rain sifted the earth as Emma fell asleep in the wee hours of the morning. The ground was covered in a dewy mist when she woke up. Spiderwebs were dotted with raindrops, and a gossamer fog blanketed the tops of the pines in the distant woods that enveloped Norwood Boyd's house. It lay atop the majestic silver maple outside her window as well.

It would be dawn soon.

Emma slid out of bed and clicked on the overhead light. She opened her suitcase and gathered the shreds of her Friend Atlas from the floor and the desk and the windowsill, from under the bed, on the bed, and everywhere they had floated and come to rest as she had cut and cut and cut the night before.

She gently spread the pieces on top of her folded clothes. They made a pile that completely covered everything under it.

She couldn't part with the atlas yet. But she didn't regret her decision to cut it to pieces. She was done with regrets. She would only look forward now. Just like Leo Cake only looked forward. *This* is our home. For *now*. Finally, she understood.

She came downstairs with her suitcase and her satchel,

dressed for the long day's ride. Her father was standing in the kitchen, confused.

"Why are there baked goods down here? We're not opening this morning!"

Arlouin held her head high and said, "Emma and I made the cake. It's our thank-you gift to a town that was good to us."

"They were *not* good to us!" said Leo Cake. He adjusted his glasses and peered more closely at the cake. He wondered what kind it was. He longed for a taste, to see if he could guess.

"They *were* good to us," said Arlouin in a matter-of-fact voice as she ushered the boys outside. "No town is perfect. No place is perfect. No day is perfect, Leo. We are not perfect people, either. And thank goodness."

Leo opened his mouth to say something and shut it instead. He looked around at the café they had created, in this town they had come to for reasons he had not understood. He shook his head and joined his family outside on the sandy lane, where the night was slowly slipping away and the sky was lightening from inkiest black to darkest gray to soft silver to a lighter hue the color of stones.

It was time to move on. Everything was in place for their move.

The Cake family folded themselves into their Ford Econoline and left, like secrets, in the night:

Emma Alabama Lane Cake
Benjamin Lord Baltimore Cake
Jody Traditional Angel Food Cake
Van Chocolate Layer Cake
Roger Black Forest Cake
and
Gordon Ridiculously Easy No-Knead Sticky
    Buns Cake.

Leo Meyer Lemon Cake was in the driver's seat.

Arlouin Hummingbird Spice Cake was in her place in the front passenger seat.

Somehow there were also four dogs.

The dogs slobbered and crammed and kissed and growled and scrabbled and shoved and collapsed themselves on top of their Cakes, who adjusted and shifted and accommodated them as best they could.

Arlouin switched on the inside car lights—for it was not quite dawn—and pulled a map from the glove compartment. The road atlas was still missing. She handed the map to Ben.

"Navigate, please."

Ben took the map with no emotion. He and Emma exchanged a look that said nothing. No one felt a thing.

Leo Cake put the key in the ignition and the engine sputtered to life. He put the car in reverse and backed them onto the sandy lane, away from the silver maple tree. He put the car in drive and began to ease forward.

And then Gordon, suddenly coming to life for all of them, said, "Hey! There's something in that tree! In that hole, in that tree! It's pink!"

Dear Emma,

It's me, your friend "To Whom It May Concern."

Miss Eula was at her Eastern Star meeting until late last night (she plays the piano and they had a singathon), so I couldn't talk to her until early this morning—and I do mean early. She called Mr. Butterfield, who is always up before dawn with the roosters, before he goes to work at his law office, and he said she can borrow his chicken wagon/coop. So we are headed over to Norwood Boyd's as soon as the sun is up, because that's when the chickens wake up.

"No time like the present," says Miss Eula, "for chickens, for gardens, and for friends!"

So COME OVER TO NORWOOD BOYD'S!

I can't wait for you to see the chickens in action.

Your Friend (probably your best friend EVER),
Ruby L. (To Whom It May Concern)

～ Chapter Thirty-Eight ～

"I have to say good-bye to Ruby!" Emma was out of the car—everyone was out of the car. Even the dogs were out of the car.

"We have no time for good-byes, Emma," said her father.

"I'll make it short!"

"Short, long, we don't have time!" Leo had tried good-byes himself, when he was a boy. It was torture. He didn't want to remember those times. He had done a good job of forgetting them. "We need to go," he insisted. "We need to get on the road. We have hundreds of miles to cover today."

"Nobody got to say good-bye," said Jody.

"Yeah," complained Van. "Nobody. And the team will be here soon. Can't we wait until then?"

"I want to stay here!" whined Roger.

"Me too!" said Gordon. "I don't want to move!" He began to cry.

Gordon was wearing Eudora Welty's old tutu. He had packed his white one in his suitcase. Arlouin picked him up and shushed him. She looked at her husband.

Emma shook her head. "I'll leave! I promise I'll leave, Daddy. But you have to take me to say good-bye to Ruby.

She's done so much for me, and I didn't even get to thank her. She's helping me make a garden right now!"

"What?" said Leo Cake. "You know better than to start something you can't finish, Emma." He was using his stoic voice, the one he used when he didn't want to have a conversation. Yes, he remembered the times when he was a boy and wanted to stay, and he remembered how he learned to be dispassionate and matter-of-fact. The success of their moves depended on it. His father had taught him that.

"Let's go," he commanded. "In the car."

Arlouin made no move to get in the car. "Where is this garden, Emma?" she asked, even though she had read the note and knew where the garden was. "Is it at Ruby's?" She would give her daughter a chance to make her case.

"No," said Emma, "but it's not far from here. We could drive there on the way out of town. Please, Daddy! I'm not asking to stay. I'm just asking to say good-bye."

"No," said Leo. He opened the driver's door of the car.

"Is it a *secret garden*?" Arlouin asked in her most pointed voice. She stared at Emma as if to say, *I'm trying to help you here!*

Emma blinked. *The Secret Garden* was a book.

"Yes!" said Ben, stepping in for his sister. Everyone looked at Ben. "Well, I know about it, too," he said. "So it's not so secret, I guess."

"Gaaaa!" said Leo Cake. But he hesitated at the car door.

"And there are chickens!" said Emma, feeling her father's hesitation. "They are over there now, eating up the weeds and fixing the ground so we can plant in the garden, and I don't know if they'll even keep doing it after we move, but it's okay if they don't. I just want to say thank you to Ruby—and Miss Eula!—thank you so much for trying, and . . . and . . . for being my friend, maybe my best friend ever, and . . . and . . ."

Emma burst into tears. She had fought so hard not to feel anything last night, or this morning, but now she was lost in her feelings again, and in her chest was a pounding—*Mine! Mine! Mine!* Memories of her house—*my house*—filled her senses, and it was way too much for one eleven-year-old heart to endure.

Arlouin started crying while holding the crying Gordon. She pulled from the waistband of his tutu an oversize Snowberger's handkerchief that Mary Wilson had given him and wiped her eyes. Gordon took it and blew his nose.

Leo shoved up his glasses with a moan. This leaving got harder every time they did it, and this time was the worst. It was insurrection, that's what it was. And yet, these were his people and he was in charge. Just like his father, Archibald, had been in charge when it had been the two of them on the road for so many years. They were itinerant bakers! A noble and proud profession. Citizens of the World!

Somebody had to be in charge. *Somebody* had to make the decisions.

He softened his voice for his people.

"It will be better when we are gone and down the road."

And then Emma made a decision of her own. From deep inside herself she made her stand.

"I won't go down the road," she said, "unless I can say good-bye to Ruby first." She shivered as an army of anxious prickles raced across her shoulders and down her back.

"Me, neither," said Ben. He swallowed and stood up straight. He was tall for his age and almost eye-to-eye with his father.

Ben's bravery buoyed Emma.

"You'll have to pick me up and force me into the car."

"Emma!" said her mother.

"You'll have to catch me first," said Ben, equally emboldened.

"Yeah!" said the rest of the Cake boys in unison.

"Well," said Leo. There were a lot more of them than there were of him. But that wasn't the point. He looked at the earnest faces of his wife and children in the last of the predawn light. Then a clutch of crows called and swooped from the tall pines in the woods and it was morning. Just like that.

Leo Cake made a decision. He narrowed his eyes and used his most serious voice.

"Do you promise you'll behave after we go to this garden and say good-bye? Do you promise—all of you!—you'll get back in the car and go down the road without complaint?"

"Yes," said Emma immediately, emphatically.

"And I'll say good-bye to House while Emma says good-bye to Ruby," said Ben. "He lives close to this garden. It won't take any time."

Then Ben addressed his brothers.

"I'm the oldest," he said with authority, separating himself from his brothers for good. "When you each get to be twelve, you can say good-bye to your friends in person, too. Got it?"

Jody, Van, and Roger stared at Ben, unhappy but subdued.

"And Gordon, I'll take you with me to say good-bye to Honey. Because you're the baby."

Gordon sniffed and beamed. Arlouin put him down.

The first yellow sun rays winked off the side mirror of the Ford Econoline. The sun pushed itself up and awake and began to sweep up the remains of the night's fog.

"We're decided, then," said Leo with relief. "Everybody back in the car. Emma, show me where this garden is."

~ Chapter Thirty-Nine ~

The Ford Econoline van left the sandy lane, turned onto the dirt road that bordered the ball fields, passed the Tolbert Twins' house and Cleebo's house, and came to the intersection that housed the Methodist church, the Baptist church, and all the dead Methodists and Baptists.

"Goodness," said Arlouin.

"We passed two cemeteries on the way here!" chorused Jody and Van.

"We're going the wrong way," whined Roger.

"Keep going," said Emma.

Soon they came to another intersection, another dirt road. Pine forest grew on all sides of them.

"This is the middle of nowhere," said Leo. But something felt familiar here, even though, to the unpracticed eye, it was just pine forest and dirt road.

"Turn left," said Ben.

A curve left, a curve right, and there it was, on the left in a huge clearing.

Norwood Boyd's house.

"This is it," said Emma. The lump in her throat felt too big to swallow. She took a deep breath.

"Here?" asked Leo. His voice had a catch in it.

"Whoa!" said Jody and Van and Roger in unison.

"We were here yesterday!" said Gordon.

"Yes, we were," said Emma, although it felt like a million years ago.

Leo turned off the dirt road and onto the orange-pebbled driveway that led to the tall iron gates. He stopped the car before he reached them.

"Can you drive all the way in, Daddy?" asked Emma. "I can't see the garden. I can't tell if Ruby is here."

But Leo had put the car in park. He left the engine running and got out of the car without saying a word. His every nerve was alive and alert. He staggered as if his legs weren't sure how to pick themselves up and take step after step, as if his mind were disconnected from his body.

"Shhh," said Arlouin, although no one in the car had moved or said a word. All eyes were on Leo Cake as he stood in front of the open gates and buckled softly to his knees, as if his legs had now decided to stop working altogether.

Arlouin opened her car door and moved in her own hesitant way toward her husband. "Leo? What is it? *Is it your heart?*"

It was.

Leo Cake buried his face in his hands. The Ford Econoline erupted in a spray of Cakes leaping from the car and rushing to their father, shouting and barking and circling him in a show of protection.

"Daddy?" Emma got to him first. She skidded to her

knees in front of Leo, clasped his wrists, and gently pulled her father's strong baker's hands from his stalwart, itinerant face.

"Daddy?"

Leo Cake looked with bewilderment into the anxious faces of his wife and children and then again at the ornately carved gates and the turreted weathered house beyond the gates.

"I need a minute," he said, a hoarse croak in his voice. "I'm fine. I need a few minutes, that's all."

⁓ Chapter Forty ⁓

Things happened quickly after that.

The chicken-tractor-school-bus-portable-chicken-coop arrived with Miss Eula behind the wheel, waving and hollering for Leo to move his car. Cakes scattered out of the way. Emma grabbed Gordon while Jody, Van, Roger, and Arlouin helped Leo inside the gates. Leo sat heavily on an immense old tree stump and stared at the house with its eight majestic silver maples protecting it, their branches waving in the now-insistent morning breeze.

Ben ran for the Ford Econoline. "I've got it!"

"Since when have you been driving?" shouted Arlouin.

Ben gave his mother a *let's talk about it later* wave, drove the van through the gates, and chose a spot on the grass near the house to park it.

Arlouin turned her attention to her husband. "Leo?"

"I just want to sit here a minute," he said, breathless. "Maybe many minutes."

Arlouin patted on Leo. "Take all the time you need, dear," she said. "Are you sure you're all right?"

"Daddy?" repeated Emma. She felt she shouldn't have been so insistent, so pushy, back at the bakery. Gordon, in Emma's arms, knew this wasn't the time to cry. He watched his father closely and breathed for him, in and out.

Leo gave Emma a pat. "I'm fine, Girl Scout," he said. He took Gordon from Emma and hugged him. "I'm fine," he told his youngest son. "Run and play a minute and let me get my breath back."

Arlouin shooed her children away with "Let your daddy rest!" and sat down to share the stump with her husband. She took his hand in hers and squeezed it. He squeezed back. Whatever was happening with Leo, it was something big and Arlouin would stay with him.

Spiffy, Alice, Bo-Bo, and Hale-Bopp streaked into the woods, where there were more skunks, possums, raccoons, foxes, deer, and squirrels than they would have time to chase. More pinecones than they would be able to chew. More rain puddles than they would have time to splash through. Dog heaven.

Miss Eula tooted her horn as she steered the portable chicken coop through the iron gates and around the side of the house to where the garden lay waiting.

"You Cake boys!" called Miss Eula. She was wearing a pink flowered muumuu and a ridiculously floppy straw hat. "Come help us!"

Ruby tumbled out of the chicken tractor behind her grandmother. "Yeah!" she yelled. "Come help us!" She was wearing a straw hat, too. "Where's Emma?"

Emma had left her mother and father on the wide stump at the gate and was headed toward the chicken tractor along with her brothers. But she took a detour first.

"All Cakes on Deck!" called Ben, and immediately his brothers began to help roll chicken wire where it was needed, including around the volunteer tomato plants. Miss Eula showed them how to do it, and Ruby supervised, while keeping an eye out for Emma. Where was she?

House Jackson showed up with Cleebo. They both wore baseball caps and had their gloves under their arms.

"Hey!" yelled Ben. "Great!"

Cleebo grinned wide as House waved a greeting with his good arm. "I thought we could use the help, if we're gonna make a garden out of this. I'm pretty much one-handed right now."

"So much for secrets," snapped Ruby.

"Secretly planning, publicly doing," said Ben. "I figured it out." He blushed. Ruby blushed back.

"Good, good!" said Miss Eula. "House, there's a shovel, a rake, a hoe, and some garden gloves in the bus. Go get them, please. Take Ruby with you—she can help and she knows where they are. And get my apron! It's got the clippers and scissors and what-have-yous in the pockets!"

Cleebo puffed up and began boasting immediately. "I've been here before! Ask House! I know things about this place!"

"Great," said Ruby. That braggart Cleebo. "You can take over from me!"

"Go find your friend," Miss Eula said to Ruby. "Come here, Cleebo Wilson." Cleebo groaned but did as he was told. Miss Eula sent Ben to the chicken tractor with House.

While the boys and Miss Eula quickly made the garden ready for the chickens, who were complaining loudly inside their bus, Ruby found Emma on the back porch of Norwood Boyd's house. Emma hugged Ruby fiercely when she saw her. It was a spontaneous, impulsive hug. Ruby hugged her back and shrugged off the backpack she was wearing.

"I'm so glad to see you!" Ruby said. "I was so afraid you wouldn't come. When I dropped off the note this morning, I saw your van packed to the gills and I was sure you were leaving."

"We *are* leaving," said Emma.

Ruby sighed. Without speaking, the two friends sat themselves next to each other on the top step of the porch.

"Miss Eula says we're gonna make a garden here, either way," said Ruby. "She says it's a good use of an old space that needs refreshing, and Mr. Butterfield thinks it's a great idea."

"He does?"

"Yes!" said Ruby. "Mr. Butterfield wrote Mr. Norwood's will, and he says this is a perfect idea. He called it *the symphony true*."

Ruby shrugged in a that's-that way, so Emma did, too.

"I should be helping," said Emma. "I just wanted to say good-bye to the house first. Then I'll say good-bye to your chickens."

"This old house is a real mess," said Ruby. She took off her straw hat and shoved her unruly hair out of her face. "I don't know why you got so attached to it."

"It spoke to me," Emma replied truthfully. "I can't explain it. Just like you can't explain why you think my brother is cute."

"I do not!"

"Do too."

"I've course-corrected!" sputtered Ruby.

"And I've flown to the moon!"

A temperate breeze cooled their faces as the sunshine got busy warming the day. It would be another steamy one.

"As boys go, House is kinda cute, too," said Emma.

Ruby hooted. He was. "I brought you something," she said. "I made it after I left you your mail." She unzipped her backpack and pulled out a package wrapped in brown paper and tied with a piece of twine.

"Really?" said Emma, touched. "Thank you!"

"Open it first," directed Ruby. "Then thank me. Profusely."

Emma untied the twine, opened the package, and pulled out a box filled with blank paper, stamped envelopes addressed to Ruby, and a sharpened number two pencil with a rubber eraser affixed to the top.

"Oh," Emma said. "I don't know what to say."

"*Profusely*," repeated Ruby.

Emma laughed. She would miss this girl.

"I know you like drawing," Ruby went on. "So you don't even have to write words! Just draw me something to tell me what's happening, put it in one of these envelopes, find a post office or a mailbox to stick it in, and I'll get it! Be sure to sign it. I'll write you back, if you send me an address. I'm a great letter writer."

"I see," said Emma. And she did. She wanted to hug Ruby again, but something told her that one hug a day—or maybe a year—was Ruby's limit.

A cheer rose from the direction of the garden and both girls ran to see what it was about after tucking Emma's present back inside Ruby's backpack and leaving it on the porch.

Eight chickens scrambled down the ramp at the back of the school bus—which was now inside the garden—and were happily and greedily chomping and pecking and scratching in the garden that had been prepared for them.

Leo and Arlouin were no longer on their stump. A green pickup truck crunched onto the pebbles and drove up the driveway, bobbled over a pile or two of spent kudzu, and came through the open iron gates. In the back bed, sitting on cushions and securely fastened so it wouldn't slide, was an enormous full-sheet sheet cake, enough to feed one hundred people.

Sitting in the driver's seat of the truck was Jerome Fountainbleu. "I came to the café to apologize and saw the cake!" he hollered out his open windows to no one and everyone. Behind Jerome was a caravan of cars and trucks slowly turning into the pebbled lane and driving across the front yard's freshly washed stubble of grass. The cars and trucks scattered the grasshoppers and crickets and parked under the trees, near the garden, next to the woods, wherever they could find a space.

"Good garden of peas," said Ruby. "I didn't think he was gonna *do* it!"

"What is this?" asked Emma.

"There were so many people in town so early this morning—it was weird," said Ruby. "Mr. Fountainbleu ran at the chicken wagon like a mad dog running down Main Street, and when we stopped for him, he said, 'You're their landlord! Where did they go?' and Miss Eula told him to follow her, she was heading for Norwood Boyd's."

Emma raised her eyebrows and watched the procession. People piled out of their cars. They pulled folding tables and chairs from truck beds, and began setting them up on the front lawn of Mr. Norwood Boyd's home, laughing and telling old stories, shouting *one-two-three lift!* and *whoa there!* and *back up!* and *a little help here!* and *watch your toes!*

237

"I'll be right back," said Ruby. "Let me check on the chickens."

I've got freshly pressed napkins! came from a prepared soul and *for pity's sake* from a certain crotchety soul and *bless your heart! bless your heart!* from one intrepid pie-baking soul.

This place, Emma thought. *This place.*

They were all here. They had all come. And they had brought cake.

Chapter Forty-One

Melba Jane tapped on Emma's shoulder, and Emma swung around with a start to face her. She had never seen Melba without Finesse.

"I just wanted to say hey."

"Hey," said Emma. She was sure the surprise showed on her face.

"We've got something in common," Melba told her. Then she gestured to her sisters and brothers tumbling from her mother's car. There were five of them. The tallest one ran to Melba shouting, "Score! Score! Score!"

"I'm the oldest," Melba said as George tugged on his sister's sundress. "And I've got to babysit. I just wanted to say hi."

Before Emma could answer her, Melba shoved a piece of paper into Emma's palm. "A coupon," she said. "For one free haircut at Locks by Leila. That's my mom's beauty parlor just outside of town. It's next to our house. Come anytime."

Emma smiled. "Thank you, Melba Jane."

"Don't mention it," Melba said breezily as she ran to help her mother. Now that Emma was leaving this town, there really was a friend bonanza.

Jerome Fountainbleu stood in the front yard and cried,

"Leo! Arlouin! Cakes! I'm so very sorry!" There was no answer.

Ruby ran back to Emma. "What did I miss?"

Emma stuck her coupon in her shorts pocket. "Nothing much," she said. "I can't find my parents."

"Please don't leave!" Jerome Fountainbleu implored, shouting over the heads of the growing crowd. "I was remiss! I don't know what came over me! I'm not that kind of man—really I'm not!"

"He most certainly is," said Miss Mattie Perkins as she and a host of others opened folding chairs and placed them at tables. "Sometimes he goes temporarily insane. We try not to hold it against him."

"We are all temporarily insane at one time or another," sniffed Clementine Watson.

Miss Eula found the girls and put one hand on Ruby's shoulder and another on Emma's. "Come with me," she said.

Parting Schotz supervised Lamar Lackey and Hampton Hawes as they hoisted the sheet cake and brought it to the largest folding table. It would not fit.

"Let's serve it from the back of the truck," Pip said.

"Please forgive me!" Jerome was now bellowing, arms outstretched and a pained look on his face.

"Hush!" yelled the crowd, but there was affectionate laughter to accompany their shouting.

Jerome made a quarter turn with every sentence he blustered. "Look! I've brought all your customers and then some. We want you back! We need you! No one makes cakes the way you do! Cake is important! Like pie!"

Finesse emerged from the crowd, eyeballed Ben, and smiled. *A true artist never gives up*, she told herself.

"Frances," said Pip, "put together some entertainment."

"*Tout de suite*, Poppy!" Finesse beamed. Ben could wait. She began to gather her dancers from the Aurora County All-Stars pageant. "*Vite! Vite!*"

Pip put a hand on Ben's shoulder and said, "Come with me, young man." And Ben did.

The Aurora County All-Stars spilled out of cars and trucks to the delighted cries of the Cake boys. They began a pickup game immediately in Norwood Boyd's vast back-yard, using piles of garden weeds for bases, not caring that there was an iron fence at the back of the property and the woods would swallow any hits beyond second base. Honey and Gordon positioned themselves along the third-base line and practiced twirls and jetés.

A morning picnic was in full swing.

The only thing on the menu was cake, and the mystery held in a handwritten note:

Come Now.

~ Chapter Forty-Two ~

"We should be on our way," said Leo Cake to his wife. His voice was subdued and gentle. They stood in the wide hallway of Norwood Boyd's home. House had left the blinds pulled up the day before and the sun sparkled like diamonds on this luminous summer morning. The hallway furniture and photographs were bathed in its radiance.

"I know I've been here before," Leo said softly. "In this house, in that kitchen we just walked through. In this hallway. It was a long time ago." He thought a moment more and said, "A lifetime ago."

Arlouin watched her husband as he took small side steps down the hallway, stopping with every step to push up his glasses and peer at the pictures on the walls. None of them looked familiar to him, not even the picture of young Pip in Norwood Boyd's uniform. Of course that picture would have been taken before Leo Cake was born.

"Cakes never go anywhere twice," murmured Arlouin, remembering Archibald Cake's old adage.

Leo rubbed the bottom of his chin with the backs of his fingers. "That's why I couldn't believe I'd been here before."

The back door opened and here came Pip and Miss Eula and Ruby, Emma, and Ben. Miss Mattie was close behind them. She left the back door open and the house filled with fresh air.

"Then why were you here?" asked Arlouin. "Did Archie bake here?"

"Yes," said Leo. "No. I don't remember."

"I do," said Pip. "And you will remember, too, if you allow it."

Leo shook his head ever so slightly. Was that a *no*, or was that a question?

"I'll help you," said Pip. "Norwood was in the merchant marines for many years. He was chief cook on the SS *Joshua Hendy* during World War II. The chief cook prepares the menus and meals and makes sure the kitchen has everything it needs, from meat to fruit and vegetables to desserts. Your dad, Archibald, was his baker."

"He was?" Leo's face changed. He looked twelve years old again.

"He was. And he was only nineteen. It was his first baking job, but he had been baking with his family for years, just like your children do . . . and like you did growing up with your dad, right?"

"Right," said Leo in a hesitant voice. "But we never baked on a ship."

"What about the *Mayflower*, Daddy?" Emma remembered her father's stories of the long lineage of Cakes.

"A ship needs bakers!" said Pip. "It's an itinerant job. The baker bakes all the bread and desserts, makes the salads, and the night lunches for the night crew. And your daddy, Archibald Cake, learned to make soup. He loved to make soup more than he loved to bake."

Leo's eyes flashed on Emma, and Emma took her father's hand. She held it tight.

Pip continued. "As you know, bakers aren't soup makers, but Archie was. When Norwood got sick in the Philippines, it was Archibald's soup that saved his life."

"Was it chicken soup?" asked Ruby. She was clearly not buying this story.

"Possibly," said Pip.

"Great," said Ruby.

But Emma was thrilled. "My grandfather was a soup maker!" she whispered. "Why didn't I know this?"

Pip had a ready answer. "Because he left that job after his time as a mariner was over, and he went to the next job, and he quit making soup. But he and Norwood had a bond. Archie had saved Norwood's life, and Norwood would never forget it."

"Norwood never told me this story," said Miss Mattie in a wondering voice. "I knew he was a mariner, I knew he had traveled the world, but I didn't know about Archibald, and I didn't know about . . ." She looked at Leo. ". . . you."

Leo watched Miss Mattie tear up as she shook her head.

"And we were so close." She sounded lost. "So close.

We talked all the time, especially in his last years. We were . . . close."

Miss Eula cleared her throat and said tenderly to her sister-in-law, "You weren't the only one who loved Norwood, Mattie."

Miss Mattie sniffed and wiped away a tear.

"Excuse me," she said. "It's hot in here."

Pip took over. "That's right. Archie loved Norwood, too, and came to visit him when Leo here was twelve years old."

"My age," said Ben.

"That's *right*," said Leo. His face broke into an astonished smile. "I remember. I remember!"

"And do you remember playing ball here? With me and Norwood?"

Leo let go of Emma's hand and stuck his fingers under his glasses and over his eyes for a long moment. Then he removed them and said, "Yes. Yes. I remember. I remember it all."

Leo paced the hall. Arlouin gently pinched her lips with the fingers of her right hand and watched him.

"I didn't want to leave here," Leo said, still pacing, memory flooding him like a sun that had been too long eclipsed by the moon. "I *loved* it here. I knew my father did, too. *We* loved it. We were here for a long time."

Leo swallowed the tears in his throat. "I begged to stay," he said, the words coming in a rush. "Begged. This house

245

spoke to me. This place was the one where we would stay forever. I hated moving. Hated it."

Emma's heart began to pound hard in her chest. She had trouble breathing. She dared not speak.

"But my father said no, we needed to move on. There was a bakery waiting for us; there were people to help. This was just a visit . . . and that's when I stopped hoping."

Ben had been listening intently, his own hope climbing despite himself. "If your father loved Norwood Boyd, why did he leave?" he asked.

"Because it's what we do," said Leo.

"It doesn't have to be," said Miss Eula.

"Who wrote the note?" asked Arlouin.

"Archie did," said Pip.

⌐ *Chapter Forty-Three* ⌐

"Archie?" asked Leo. "How can that be? He's been gone twelve years. He died soon after Ben was born."

"We never knew him," said Emma.

"Archie wrote the note when you and he were here, Leo," said Pip, "when you were twelve. He couldn't stop traveling, he said—it was in his blood and circumstances were what they were then—but maybe you could, he said.

"The letter was to be sent to you when you had a twelve-year-old child, if you ever did, to help remind you of what it felt like to want to stay. Sometimes I think Norwood stayed alive long enough to send it to you, Leo. You and Archie meant that much to him."

"But how did he know about my family?" asked Leo.

"Archie and Norwood wrote letters to each other for decades," explained Pip. "Archie wrote Norwood when his first grandson, Ben, was born."

"That's me," said Ben.

"That's you," said Miss Eula.

"Oh my goodness," said Arlouin.

"And now," said Miss Mattie, having recovered herself, "we're going to give your father some air. We're going to give *me* some air. I did not know this part of the story any more than you did," she told Emma and Ruby and Ben.

To Miss Eula she said, "I'm not a bitter person, Eula. And when I'm wrong, I say so. You could have told me why you were renting to the Cakes instead of giving me the storage space."

"What would have been the fun in that?" asked Miss Eula. Her eyes twinkled. "Pip still picks up Norwood's mail. He told me Leo had answered the note, so I wrote to say I had space for rent, and we went from there."

"You could have told me," complained Miss Mattie.

"It wasn't my story to tell," said Miss Eula. "Take these children outside, Mattie."

"I don't want to go," Emma protested.

"Go, honey," said her father. "We'll be there directly."

"Come on, little sister," said Ben, suddenly so much older. He held out his hand and Emma took it. They exchanged a look of solidarity. Then Emma held out her other hand for Ruby. Ruby eyeballed it for a long moment and then shook it.

Miss Mattie harrumphed and led Emma, Ben, and Ruby through the kitchen and out the back door.

"Think I'll go, too," said Pip. "There's a party outside, and I hear there's cake—your cake."

"There is?" Arlouin stepped into the living room and saw the life teeming outside the grand front window. How could they not have heard it? The sounds of the world began to filter back to them. "Look, Leo! They've come to see us off!"

"They've come to ask you to stay," said Pip. "The house is yours if you want it. It's been arranged."

Leo's heart beat a steady *thump-thump-thump* in his ears. He didn't know what to say.

"You'll find yourself in this house, if you look," said Pip.

He stepped smartly to the back door and called to the Aurora County All-Stars, "Play ball!" and the air filled with wild cheering.

∽ Chapter Forty-Four ∽

"You can imagine a man like me settling down . . . it's a frightful thought," said Leo Cake. He sat on a settee in the hallway. Arlouin sat next to him.

"I can imagine," she said.

Miss Eula stood in the middle of the hallway looking at photos. "There I am as a young bride," she said. "And there's Mattie with Norwood—she never could get him to fall in love with her the way she was with him. She tried, poor soul. It broke her heart. But they *were* fast friends to the end."

"I have friends everywhere," said Leo in a soft voice.

"Are you leaving?" asked Miss Eula.

"I don't know what to do now," said Leo, honestly.

"You can't run away from your heart by going somewhere else," said Miss Eula. "I found that out the hard way, too. You suit up and you show up right here, every day. With those who love you."

"But we're itinerant bakers!" said Leo. "A noble and proud profession. Citizens of the World!"

"The itinerant world will come to you," said Miss Eula.

"There is so much need in the world, after all," mumbled Leo, remembering his father's words, "and cake is one simple way to soothe it."

"Sometimes we are needed right where we are," said Arlouin.

"Staying put is an art," affirmed Miss Eula. "And speaking of staying put, I have some chickens to attend to." She left Leo and Arlouin alone in the long hallway of Norwood Boyd's house.

"I remember," said Leo. "He wanted a family."

"Who?"

"Norwood Boyd. And he created one. All those letters, all those people who loved him." Leo wiped a tear from his cheek. "Did I love him?"

"Let's get some air, Leo," said Arlouin.

They stood on the back porch watching the exuberance around them:

Ruby borrowed Cleebo's catcher's mitt. Ben and House reorganized everyone into teams. Cleebo's father, Woodrow "Pete" Wilson, joined in, as did Lamar Lackey and even House's father, Leonard Jackson.

"Want to play, Mattie?" called Pip.

"I'd sooner chew broken glass," said Miss Mattie.

"Wait for me!" called Ferrell Ishee, Halleluia School's fourth-grade teacher. His daughter, Spud, danced with Gordon and Honey on the third-base line.

Finesse tapped Ben on the arm. "I leave in three weeks for the Lanyard School and it would be untoward of me to lead you on in a romance. *Quel dommage.*"

"Okay," said Ben. His face went beet red. Cleebo cackled from his pile of pokeweed at first base.

"He's a blockhead!" shouted Emma from home plate.

"*Très bien,*" said Finesse. She sashayed away, looking back now and then, to make sure Ben was watching.

The chickens made a racket, clucking contentedly in the garden. Ruby's mother, Evelyn Lavender, county extension agent, had arrived to watch their progress so far. "You don't need much to garden," she was saying to a clutch of folks eating cake near the garden gate. "Just some seeds and some sweat."

"And some chickens!" Miss Eula chimed in. She fanned herself with her straw hat. The day was heating up, and it wasn't yet eight o'clock.

Emma stood next to Ruby near the pokeweed home plate.

"Maybe you won't need that present I gave you after all," Ruby said.

Emma shook her head. "We always move." She was resigned to it now. She couldn't risk hope. After all, Archibald Cake had moved, anyway.

"Keep it," Ruby said, "and be sure to sign all your drawings, so I can sell them when you get famous!"

Emma smiled. "You'll be famous before I am."

Ruby hooted. "I'm already famous! Everybody in this town knows who *I* am!"

"I think you mean infamous," said Emma.

Now it was Ruby's turn to laugh.

Spiffy, Alice, Bo-Bo, and Hale-Bopp came bounding—or trotting, in Spiffy's case—back from the woods covered in leaves and burrs and pine straw and mud and spider-webs and happiness. They insinuated themselves into the makeshift game.

On the porch, Arlouin Cake, who understood a thing or two about the importance of traditions, kissed her sweet husband on the cheek and said, "I'm going to go slice cake. We have never left the cake-slicing duties to others! I'm not going to start now. And someone has to make sure those dogs don't create chaos."

Leo gave his wife a startled look. Tears crowded Arlouin's eyes. "No matter what comes," she said to her Leo, "we are in this together."

She held her head high and walked briskly down the back-porch steps and away to the front yard where the cake was already half gone. Jerome Fountainbleu was so glad to see her he almost collapsed.

A car radio began to blast "Act Naturally," and a host of cake eaters laughed and sang along. Finesse had assembled them and now she directed them, her hips and arms waving wildly and her blue-tipped hair bobbing in time to the music.

"Glory be," said Dot Land as she thought about the mail every one of her neighbors treasured, and the mail delivered to Norwood Boyd over the years, and the years he had chosen to live alone. "I renew my commitment to correspondence," she whispered.

"Good thing," said Carl Fontana, next to her.

And Phoebe "Scoop" Tolbert? Phoebe was at home, with her phone off the hook, with her bobby-pinned hair in its TP tent, fast asleep.

As the happy clangor captured the day, Ruby squatted at home plate and caught Cleebo's pitches. Emma stood a few feet away and studied her father standing on the back porch by himself.

She tried to imagine him here at her age—Ben's age, really—and she wondered how it must feel to be all grown-up and back in a place you loved when you were a child, back in the place that spoke to you and called you back, even when you hadn't known it.

What was it like to push that longing out of your memory, to a place where it no longer existed? She had been ready to do that herself. She shuddered to think of it now.

Leo Cake stood very still and soaked it all in. The smells of the sweat and tears and triumphs of these people, and the sights and sounds of their awkwardness and willingness, their friendliness, their fighting. All the things that make up a family.

A million years had passed since he had wanted to belong here. He didn't know if he *could* stay, even if he wanted to. If Archibald hadn't been able to stay, how could he change that?

The temperate breeze fluttered the leaves of the majestic silver maples that surrounded Norwood Boyd's house. Then it found Leo on the porch and cradled him in its sweet embrace. It felt so much like Archie's arms around him, so long ago, that Leo trembled in recognition.

Then he closed his eyes and opened his heart.

Emma felt the familiar sweet breeze, too. She crossed the yard to where her father stood.

"Please," Leo whispered, the same way he had uttered it when he was twelve years old, on this same back porch. The breeze danced, the leaves fluttered, the chickens squawked. The radio played and the revelers feasted and frolicked.

Then Leo Cake slowly opened his eyes.

Emma smiled at her father.

Leo smiled at Emma Lane Cake, his daughter.

Yes.

∽ *Epilogue* ∽

They would find it the next day in the hallway of the old house.

An older man with a look of delight on his face, standing next to a beaming younger man who is holding a birthday cake with twelve candles on it. A high-spirited young boy—twelve years old, to be exact—stands with the two men, a wide grin traveling across his face, a baseball glove under his arm, his glasses slipping down his nose.

Their smiles are incandescent. Effervescent. They are so happy to be in this moment, all three of them together, a family.

At the bottom of the photograph is written in a flowing blue script,

Archibald Cake and Leo

And under that, a line from a poem by Walt Whitman, Norwood Boyd's favorite poet:

Day by day and night by night
we were together—
all else has long been
forgotten by me.

Emma's room was in the turret.

✑ Author's Note ✑

The populated world has always been filled with itinerant merchants who have traveled from place to place to sell their goods and skills. For centuries, all across the globe, these peddlers tramped dusty, rutted roads and forest paths, paddled wooden boats down rivers, trekked through mountain passes, cameled across vast deserts, or rumbled over grassy prairies, moving from settlement to hamlet to village, sometimes alone, sometimes in caravans or wagon trains, as they came to trade in the next town and the next.

They brought with them faraway, hard-to-come-by items: oranges, nuts, spices, thread, fabric, sugar, coffee, elixirs, tools . . . and crusty, yeasty bread baked in an oven built on the spot with available clay and straw or stones and earth, or a cauldron covered with coals from the fire, with the temperature and recipe precisely gauged and controlled by an expert baker.

Many of these goods are easily found in Miss Mattie's Mercantile today, or in your neighborhood stores, but years ago, towns depended on their itinerant merchants in much the same way stores wait for delivery trucks now.

These peddlers were warmly welcomed for not only the goods they carried but for the news of the outside world they brought with them. Often there were itinerant jesters or storytellers or song singers, or whole theater troupes moving from place to place, sleeping in makeshift shelters until it was time to move on.

When bakeries were established in early cities, they were often built on the outskirts of town for fear of fire. Bakers came into town with their carts piled high with bread to sell. If the baker had a family, the entire family was involved in the hard work of baking and then selling door-to-door or in a marketplace each day, much like every Cake is involved in their family business.

As towns grew and prospered, itinerant merchants and tradespeople often settled there. Sometimes they were viewed with suspicion and their motives were questioned, as they had no kin or acquaintances in their chosen home and no history with the town's inhabitants. Therefore, according to mistrustful townsfolk, they had no good reason to stay. Sometimes those vagabonds were indeed swindlers, but more often they were ready, as the world changed and became more connected, to make a permanent home. "The stranger comes to town" is an ancient story still told today, and is part of the Cakes' journey as well.

Today, itinerant workers with specialized jobs may travel with carnivals or bring their tools with them to construction sites or engineering projects. They might set up pop-up shops or trunk shows or trade exhibitions or

Christmas tree lots—or a temporary storefront. A bakery, perhaps.

Merchant mariners (who are never called sailors) are itinerant as well, and make their homes on their ships, if they are crewing deep-sea vessels. They also operate tugboats, ferries, dredges, barges, and towboats along many US waterways.

Merchant Marine tanker ships carry imports (that often end up in those delivery trucks heading for your neighborhood stores) and exports and passengers across the sea between nations during peacetime, and can be commissioned by the US Navy during wartime when they are assigned to deliver supplies and troops into war zones. Merchant Marine ships were torpedoed and shelled, and hundreds of mariners, both men and women, were prisoners of war during World War II.

Norwood Boyd is in part based on seventy-six-year-old James A. Logan, a fifty-year veteran of the Merchant Marines and chief cook on the SS *Joshua Hendy*.

From "The Log of the West Coast Maritime Industries" Vol. 30 No. 7 July 1944:

> More cooks and bakers are urgently needed by the Merchant Marine, especially men with the spirit and talents of men like James A. Logan, 76, who is rounding out half a century of seafaring. Logan is now presiding over the

galley of the SS Joshua Hendy, last reported somewhere in the Mediterranean.

The master of the Liberty ship, Captain William F. Barry of Seattle Washington, addressed the following letter to the War Shipping Administration recently:

On board this vessel I have as chief cook James A. Logan, a veteran of 49 years at sea. His food is varied, carefully and tastefully prepared and attractively served. He runs a spotless galley like clockwork. Logan works wholeheartedly to conserve food, saves and flattens every tin can, renders out every bit of fat for grease, and discards nothing. He always has time to have a bit of cake or cookie for the crew, merchant or armed guard at coffee time and I have never heard a complaint of any sort about the feeding on board. Moreover, his ration cost is well below the average for the United States-operated vessels.

The important thing about Logan is that he could well afford to spend his remaining days quietly ashore but he prefers to do his bit where he can best serve.

As the ship's baker, Archibald Cake would have been the "second cook" in the steward department, working under the chief cook and chief steward.

The word *itinerant* is derived from the Latin *iter*, meaning *way* or *journey*. I wanted to write about the journey we all take, no matter who we are or what our circumstance. All over the world humans journey, sometimes outward, sometimes inward, sometimes both. We can live in a generational homeplace or be itinerant. Maybe we are migrants, or nomads, or refugees—sometimes we are all these astonishments in a lifetime.

We wander and we experience. We run from, we run to. We welcome and we reject. We forget and we remember. We leave and we return. We strive and we lift up others in the struggle.

Each day we begin again in our quest to be safe, to be loved, to belong, and to find home.

And if we are lucky, there is cake.

Simple, Classic, Melt-In-Your-Mouth White Cake

with cloudburst vanilla frosting
(we're talking all white, like a snowstorm)

From the Cake Family Cake Archive original recipe by
Leita White-Cake-Is-My-Favorite Cake
recipe adapted with plenty of step-by-step
instructions by Emma Alabama Lane Cake with help
from Ruby Lavender

This is a three-layer cake perfect for parties of any kind or for eating in thick slices after baseball practice. It will make 24 cupcakes if you prefer cupcakes, but we really like layer cake around here.

Pay attention to your mixing technique and be sure to measure properly. Then your white cake will be both elegant and toothsome, with a perfect vanilla flavor. You don't need a box mix when you've got a cake this simple to put together. A cake made from scratch tastes better and is a lot more satisfying to make and eat.

Equipment You Will Need
(for both the cake and the frosting):

- 3 cake pans, 8" rounds are best
- 2 mixing bowls, one for dry ingredients, and one for wet
- 1 small bowl in which to capture egg yolks (you will only use the whites)
- 1 small bowl for the egg whites
- An electric hand mixer or stand mixer with beaters
- A rubber spatula for scraping the bowls
- A wooden spoon just in case
- Measuring cups and spoons
- A sifter, if you have one (if not, a fork will do)
- A 1 cup glass measuring cup
- A small spoon or fork for stirring now and then (see instructions)
- A paper bag or parchment paper to line the cake pans with
- A pair of scissors with which to cut the paper
- A pencil for drawing around the pans on the paper before you cut it
- An oven for baking the layers

- Hot pads or oven mitts and a dish towel or two for convenience
- A sink for crashing the dishes
- A plate or paper bag for each layer as it waits for frosting
- OR a cake rack for cooling
- A kitchen knife or metal spatula for frosting your cake
- A toothpick, maybe several
- A cake plate or a cake stand for your finished cake
- 1 grown-up who will open hot oven doors, fix the mixer when it goes haywire, hold the sifter for you while you turn it, eyeball your measurements, break your eggs if you're queasy about getting your fingers gooey, and otherwise offer an extra pair of hands and sometimes unwanted opinions

Ingredients You Will Need For The Cake:

- 1 cup milk
- 1-1/2 teaspoons vanilla extract
- 1 cup butter, softened
- 3 cups cake flour
- 1 tablespoon baking powder
- 5 egg whites

Make the cake first.

How to Make the Cake:

BEFORE YOU GET STARTED: Take four sticks of butter (this equals two cups of butter) out of the refrigerator and put them on the counter to soften—two sticks are for the cake, and two are for the Cloudburst Frosting. If you're not going to be making Cloudburst Frosting, just take out two sticks of butter. Let them soften while you gather your equipment and ingredients, line your cake pans, and read over your recipe. Always read the whole recipe before you begin to bake. That way there are no surprises in the middle of mixing.

1. Wash and dry your hands. Put on an apron. A towel pinned around your waist or your granddad's old shirt

worn backward works as an apron if you don't have one. Thank you for that tip, Ruby Lavender.

2. Preheat your oven to 350 degrees.

3. Line the bottom of your three cake pans with paper or parchment. I cut open a bag from the Piggly Wiggly, or (unused) paper lunch bags, put the pans on the bag, draw around the bottom of them with a pencil, and then cut out the circles and place them flat on the bottom of each pan. You do not need to grease or flour your pans. The paper on the bottom will help your layers fall right out after they have cooled, especially if you have used paper bags. Find some.
    Set the pans aside.

4. Pour 1 cup of milk into the 1 cup glass measuring cup. Add the vanilla and stir with the small spoon or fork.

5. Unwrap two sticks of butter and put them in one of the mixing bowls. Beat the softened butter at medium speed with your mixer until it's creamy. Gradually add the sugar and beat until the whole thing is light as a feather and very fluffy.

6. In the second mixing bowl, sift together the cake flour and baking powder. If you have no sifter, use a fork to

fluff it all together and mix it well. Then add the flour and baking powder mix to the butter mixture alternately with your milk mixture, beginning and ending with the flour mixture. So add a bit of flour mix, a bit of milk, repeat until you finish with the flour mix. Beat at low speed just until blended after each addition. Don't beat it up but make sure everything is blended in.

7. Separate the five eggs. Carefully crack each egg in half at the middle (tapping it smartly against the side of a bowl works well) and (also carefully) separate the shell into two halves, using your thumbs. Keep the yolk in one half of the eggshell while you let the white slip into a small bowl beneath the egg. Your fingers will get messy but you can wash them later.

   Gently plop the yolk into the other half eggshell and let more white fall into the small bowl. Do this, back and forth for each egg until you have all the whites in the bowl. Put each yolk in another bowl, cover it, put it in the refrigerator, and save your yolks for another cake or to add to scrambled eggs the next morning.

   This step may be hard at first, but it just takes practice. Soon you will ace it and teach your best friend how to do it.

8. Use a dishcloth to wipe clean your flour-mix bowl (it's empty now), and put your egg whites in it (alternatively, you can just crack the eggs over this bowl and put all the whites in it, as long as you have a clean, empty bowl when you start). Beat the egg whites at medium speed until they form stiff peaks. How to know you have beat the eggs into stiff peaks: turn off the mixer and lift the beaters up and down several times in the egg whites. The white tips should look like one of the spiky hairdos at Pip's. If they aren't spiky enough, beat a little more. They'll get there.

9. Use your rubber spatula to fold your egg whites into the batter you've prepared. *Fold* means just that. Tuck in your egg whites, like they're going to bed and you're pulling the covers up with the batter. Work in a big circle, up and over and down and up. Turn the bowl each time you fold. Do it several times. Be gentle.

10. When you've got everything folded in and it's all one color, pour your batter into the three 8" pans. Try to put roughly the same amount of batter into each pan. Use the rubber spatula to get all the batter out of the bowl. Put the pans in the preheated oven, on the same rack and not touching, and put the timer on for 20 minutes.

11. When the timer goes off, check the layers by seeing if a toothpick inserted into the middle of one comes out clean. The sides of the cake should also pull away from the pan a little bit. If the cake isn't quite done all the way through, run it back in the oven for 3 or 4 more minutes, but don't overcook.

12. Remove the cake from the oven, and let it cool in the pans for about an hour. It will sigh and pull itself together in the pan and continue cooking gently as it cools. Then, run your kitchen knife inside the pan and around the edges of the cake, to make sure none of the sides have stuck to the cake pan.

13. Using an oven mitt, turn the cake pan upside down and give it a crack onto a plate or a cooling rack, whichever you have. Don't break the plate—you can crack the pan onto the counter and "catch" the layer as it falls out. (This is one reason you want to leave it in the pan for an hour.) If you use a plate, put parchment paper or wax paper on it so the layer doesn't stick to the plate.

14. When the layers are completely cool, you can slowly peel off the paper on the bottom of each layer and then frost the layers with the Cloudburst Vanilla

Frosting that you will make next—if you haven't eaten the cake already. I'm looking at you, Ruby Lavender.

Ingredients You Will Need For The Cloudburst Frosting:

- 1 cup butter, softened (two of the sticks you took out of the fridge earlier)
- 1/4 teaspoon salt
- 1 (32 ounce) package powdered sugar
- 6 to 7 tablespoons milk (whole is best)
- 1 tablespoon vanilla extract (real vanilla extract will make a big difference)

How to Make the Frosting:

1. You can use one of your cake mixing bowls, because you washed them while the cake was baking, right?

2. In a mixing bowl, beat your now-softened butter and salt together at medium speed with the hand or stand electric mixer for 1 to 2 minutes or until dreamy-creamy.

3. Gradually add the powdered sugar alternately with the milk. So a little powdered sugar, a little milk, back and forth. Keep beating at low speed while you are doing this. (A stand mixer really helps, because you'll have two free hands.)

4. Stir in the vanilla. I like to reserve one of my tablespoons of milk to add in after I add the vanilla. Either way is fine. If you added it all in step 3, that's okay. If your frosting feels too stiff, you can add a little more milk and beat the mixture on low speed until it's the consistency you like. Trust your instincts here. You don't want it so gloopy it will slide off the sides of your cake.

5. Now you are ready to ice your cake! Frosting a cake is part art, part skill. But don't worry about it. Every cake looks great after it's frosted. Start with the bottom layer. Put it in the middle of your cake plate. Using a spoon as a scoop, top the layer with frosting. Use a kitchen knife or metal cake spatula to smooth the frosting across the top.

    Add the next layer and top it with frosting. Add the final layer and top it as well. I often stop frosting here because I like the sides without frosting. If you aren't frosting the sides, you can put lots of frosting between layers. If you are frosting the sides, make sure you put less frosting between layers. Your eye will tell you what to do.

Don't forget to lick the beaters, the spatula, and the bowl when you are done, if the rest of your family doesn't get to them first. Store your cake covered with a cake pan lid or make a tent over it with aluminum foil. It will stay fresh for about three days. But it won't last that long.

"Bon appétit!" as Finesse would say.

⌁ Acknowledgments ⌁

To be back in Aurora County, Mississippi, again is a pleasure as sweet as a four-layer Lane cake. *Love, Ruby Lavender* first appeared in print in 2001, after a ten-year wasteland of rejections (of many a manuscript) followed by five years of hilariously flattening hard labor, on both our parts, as I learned how to write a novel with Liz Van Doren at Harcourt Books. So I'm indebted to Liz for seeing the possibilities in the original picture-book world of Halleluia, Mississippi, and a little girl's love for her grandmother and all things Southern in *Love, Ruby Lavender*.

Each Little Bird That Sings followed *Ruby*, and *The Aurora County All-Stars* followed *Little Bird*. An Aurora County universe was born, which surprised us all, and now here comes Emma Lane Cake with her story and *A Long Line of Cakes* to astonish us once again.

Ardent thanks to Scholastic Press for the opportunity to revisit Aurora County with a brand-new story and a return to familiar characters loved by me and by the readers who discovered Aurora County as kids; who, as parents and teachers, shared the books with young readers; who included them in Battles of the Books, on state book award lists, and as school and community one-book projects; and who welcomed me to their schools and libraries and bookstores and fed me (often literally!) with their delight in these characters and their stories. What an adventure it has been!

Thank you to my editor David "Babka" Levithan for saying yes, and for shepherding this book into print. His thoughtful questions, along with our conversations and shared enthusiasms for Emma's story, have made me a better writer. Thanks to everyone at Scholastic for offering me a haven in which to shelter, and the spaciousness from which to create. I appreciate all of you.

The measure, pour, and bake of partnership is important to me, so I especially thank Steven Malk for nineteen years of a cup of this, a pinch of that, stir vigorously.

Thank you, Janie Kurtz, for those read-aloud days in May. Thanks to Michael Hill for the loan of his lovable canines. Bless you, Roger Purser, for sharing your many talents and for allowing me to use the names of your rowdy brothers in this book. Rest in peace, gentle spirit.

I wrote this story while pulling loaves of memory and imagination from the shelves of a sturdy baker's rack held in place by a wildly generous, completely unhinged, totally together, unwavering-in-their-love-for-me family, both chosen and inherited. Here is all my love back to you, layers upon layers. I know how lucky I am.